HEXIS

CHARLENE ELSBY

"We call a *hexis* (1) a kind of activity of the haver and the had— something like an action or movement. When one thing makes and one is made, between them there is a making; so too between him who has a garment and the garment which he has there is a *hexis*. This sort of having, then, evidently we cannot *have;* for the process will go on to infinity, if we can have the having of what we have. (2) '*Hexis*' means a disposition according to which that which is disposed is either well or ill disposed, either in itself or with reference to something else, e.g. health is a *hexis*; for it is such a disposition. (3) We speak of a *hexis* if there is a portion of such a disposition; therefore the excellence of the parts is a *hexis*."

Aristotle, *Metaphysics*

ONE

I FOLLOWED the taillights of the car ahead with the same thought I always had: if something suddenly appeared on the road, the car ahead would be the first to hit it. I would see the taillights suddenly decrease in velocity, and then I would do the same. Without staring at those taillights, I would have trouble driving after dark. When there was no car ahead, I was the one responsible for noticing when someone or something suddenly appeared. But that wouldn't happen this time, since I was following the car ahead.

The problem with any good plan is temporality. That's what it always came down to. The story would go fine without it. After eighteen years, we reunited, it would say. He confessed that he had never been able to love anyone like he had once loved me, and I allowed him the opportunity to prove himself, to show me what it would be like, now that he had changed—now that he had grown. We were so young then, with so much to learn. Just have a coffee and let me show you, he said. Of course I would; I practically had to. I would go to the coffee shop and drink a coffee. It's a thing that I did. If he were there too, drinking coffee, and happened to be talking, I couldn't help but listen. So of course I would. There was basically no way around it.

It would make up for the last time I had met him for coffee. That story went differently. After two years, we reunited. He explained how he had never been able to love anyone like he had once loved me, and I didn't believe that, because I didn't believe he had had the opportunity to meet anyone who might have been my equal. If he believed he had, and that he had failed to love that person, then he would be wrong. He had underestimated me, as he always did, as he always made sure I knew. Once I forgave him for fucking that girl, he went on about his new interests—something about role playing with his friends in a woodland setting. But that was then.

I knew the meeting wouldn't go well. I had a gash on my head from a tree branch I had met the weekend before, drinking in the woods with my new friends—better friends—but I came anyway. I put a hat over it and knew that he wouldn't notice, even though my eye sagged a little from the swelling. It was a borrowed hat—a black bucket hat from a few years before. It wasn't exactly still popular in 2001, but I forgave him, and he felt better. He would be able to go on, he said, what with my having forgiven him, and with the hope that I might someday love him again. I wouldn't.

I wasn't quite sure what I expected from him, this time. Well, that's not exactly true. I expected him to act and look exactly like he did when he was seventeen, the last time I had seen him. He had emailed me a few years after that, but he had never sent a picture, and the image I had of him was of a skinny but broad-shouldered teenager with dark blond, close-cropped curly hair, dimples and bags around his eyes from not sleeping, never sleeping. His blue eyes seemed to bug out of his head when compared to the bags around them, but they didn't go away, not even when he did sleep, which I had seen him do. He had lied about never sleeping. I would somehow tell him about all of the ways what he had done to me had affected me, my then-future relationships, my relationships with men in particular, and with women too. He would achieve an intuitive insight that encapsulated eighteen years' of what it was like to know too much about what men are capable of, and he would *make it better*. That was the most difficult part, I thought, when I imagined what would happen, but I figured that part wasn't up to me. Just as he had broken it, he would make it better. I would achieve some insight that negated eighteen years of bad habits, and I would *go on*. That part was the other difficult part. *Make it better, go on.*

The difficult part was the temporal part. That was both the immediate difficulty and the threat of the future becoming the present. It wasn't and wouldn't be as I imagined it. I didn't manage to get a word in. Well, that was an exaggeration, but I didn't get in a meaningful word. That was true enough— not in the sense that the words that I said didn't have any meaning at all, but in the sense that the words I said were not the ones that I had purposively set out to say. They were accidental words, with meaning, but not meaningful, and that was fine, because "meaning" has those two different senses that mean that saying as much does not entail any kind of contradiction. Perhaps I would do better to use other

words, just in case someone thought I had accidentally said something profound. That was all fine. I
did not tell him that I had sex with men in order to
avoid their having sex with me. I didn't get the
chance.

And now I was following him. He had told me all
about the time it had taken him to heal, how he
didn't know how it was he had made it through all of
those years, and how difficult it had been, and how
he thought it would all be worth it if only he ended
up being the sort of man I would come to love, and
how he thought it was finally time to tell me all of
this. And I got caught up in it, too. I knew I would
and that I would have to guard against that, and now
I had just gotten caught up in it. I reassured him;
everything was fine. I was getting along fine—swimmingly, even. He should have known something was
off when I used the word "swimmingly", but he
didn't seem to catch that. He didn't seem to care. I
wondered how he could embody such a contradiction—at the same time thinking that I alone could
assuage whatever it was he thought he had suffered,
that I alone could save him, and also not manage to
differentiate me in anyway from anyone else. I was
one and anyone, and he knew me as both.

If it weren't for the temporality of the thing. This
was the dangerous part, the part that got in the way
of everything, where I actually had to drive from one
part of town to another, he in his car, I in mine, eye
and mind, and when I had time to think about these
things. It was a five-minute drive, he said. We could
continue our conversation at his house, so I wouldn't
feel so badly about taking up the table at the busy
coffee shop when I didn't want to order another
coffee. I had thought I would leave, but he said there

was more work to be done, more to say, more to accomplish today, and it would only take a little longer, at his house. If it weren't for the temporality of the thing, I could say that after eighteen years, we had a lovely coffee, finally got some closure on a few matters, and that everything was wrapped up in a neat little static package that existed in two states: wrapped and unwrapped. No one accounted for the time that the package had spent wrapped or how long it took to unwrap it; there was no intermediate stage of wrapped-unwrappedness that *I* knew existed, because dichotomies are a thing created by humans and not by a temporal nature that constantly defied them. It was wrapped and then unwrapped and each of those states occupied an eternity and no time at all.

I, however, could not spend five minutes driving to his house without determining several things: he was the same, I was the same, and this time it would be different.

I considered turning off the road, just turning off the road and going home. He would knowingly consider the possibility that I had seen through him this time, and that I finally made my escape at the proper time, instead of too late. He would curse and shout, *foiled again!* before resuming his path to his house and setting down to continuing whatever it was he was doing with his life. He was supposed to have been a doctor.

I considered honking at him until he stopped, waiting until he got out of his car, and then under the watchful eyes of about twenty neighbourhood snoops I just knew lived wherever it was I was, I would explain to him that he had made a terrible mistake, I was not the kind of woman he thought I was, if he even thought I was a woman at all, and I would, securely gazed upon by those neighbours, tell him that I would never forgive him and that I secretly hoped that one day, when they weren't looking, he would think about this moment and kill himself.

Finally, I recognized the old neighbourhood. *He must still live there.* And as soon as I thought it, I also thought, *no.* I would not go back. *No no no no no.* There was a bridge here, and I was stopping.

As I pulled off of the road, the thought shook me that the bridge wasn't safe either. It was only about a hundred metres from the house. When he stopped to look back, he would notice my car was missing from the rear view mirror, and he would look around to see where I had went, and at the bridge, I would just appear to have stopped a little early. Perhaps I was worried that he wouldn't have an additional parking space available in the old driveway. I shouldn't say "old", since the driveway still existed, but to me it was old and would stay that way. I should have moved from the bridge but, as I noticed as I saw him get out of his car and start walking towards me, I didn't want to. I got out of the car.

"You know," he started, coming towards me, "I'll always think of you as young as you were back then," he said. "You'll always be beautiful to me," he said, as if I were no longer beautiful and should be aware of it. I smiled. "How many other men could promise you that?" This was as far as it would go. The bridge was made of cement, it seemed, or concrete? I didn't know the difference. The road blended into two high walls on either side, which blended into dual sidewalks, which were guarded on each edge by iron rails that seemed to have had the cement poured around them. They were in there, all right. I remembered how one day, when I had come to meet him at his house, I had found him naked and shivering in a blanket in the corner of his bedroom. He had jumped in the river, he said. He had jumped in the river, even though it was burgeoning on winter and the river was the only water around that hadn't frozen yet. He had jumped in the river to see what it was like, because he knew that every time he walked by the river, he could jump in it, and he thought that that day he might, and he did. I was supposed to recognize that, I had thought; it was some kind of accomplishment. It wasn't a large river, and it bent a little about twenty feet down, around the back of the yard surrounding the house.

"Have you jumped in the river lately?" I asked him.

"No, of course not," he said. "Why would you ask that?"

"Because of that day way back when," I told him.

"What?"

"When you jumped in the river."

"Why are you bringing that up?" he asked. "Can we go inside, please?"

"No," I said.

"It's kind of cold out here, I don't know if you noticed."

"You're getting in the river," I said.

"What?"

"In the river."

"You're not making any sense."

"I'm making perfect sense."

"You're really not."

"Get in the river."

He reached out to grab my arm; I was delusional now, of course, hysterical probably, and I should just get inside, but I wouldn't. I would have a bruise there, I knew, four fingers on my upper arm. He had to get in the river. I knew that it would be a difficult thing, one of the most difficult things I had done, but also that it had to be done, and that if I died trying, then I had died well, and that I couldn't go home unless he got in the river.

I thought I could use the iron rail. I walked a few steps and allowed him to drag me a little, until I thought I was close enough. I angled myself away from the centre of the bridge, arranging everything so that he would end up on the left. I figured his feet would slip out to the left a little, and so he should not be as far away from the rail as he was tall, but far enough away so that as he went down, it would hit him in the range of the head or the neck and not anywhere less important. I thought I could use the bit of ice forming on the ground against him, and when we were in position, I took an extra large step with my left foot to place it in front of his right, attempting to sweep it out from under him.

It didn't work. Instead, I went down. He assumed it was accidental and pulled me by the arm again, trying to get me upright, but I remained limp and waited for him to bend over farther, to try harder to right me, to get within range. As I kneeled on the ground, I tried to determine which point of contact with the ground would retain the most friction as I swung him towards the iron rail, and determining that it was my left knee, I hoped that it would provide stability enough when it came time to shove him.

It was almost as if it were planned by some divinity; kneeling on the ground, he bent over just enough so that his head appeared to me for a brief moment parallel with the rail, and I tried as hard as I could to provide enough lateral force to ram his head into the rail while keeping the left knee steady on the salted concrete. He yelped a little and suddenly understood what had just happened. He looked at me, red in the face, knocked me over on the sidewalk and put his knee on my chest to hold me down. "What the fuck was that?"

"You're getting in the fucking river," I told him, choking out the words. But he just picked me up by the arm again. The bruises would run together now, and it wouldn't be so obvious they were caused by such a hateful man. He tried to get me the rest of the way across the bridge, but I grabbed onto the rail with my right hand.

"You're being stupid," he said. He finally let go.

I sat down on the bridge, rethinking everything. I didn't know what would happen now that he knew what my plan was. Perhaps the time had passed, and I would just go with him, into the house, to finish the discussion we had started earlier. The thought of it revolted me. I started digging around in my pockets to see what I could find. I thought he might think I was looking for something important, and I was, which made it believable. I found a pen—and not just any pen. I was pretty sure this one was metal. I had stolen it from someone very important.

"Sit down with me a second," I said, trying to make it seem as though it were the most natural thing in the world, the two of us, in our thirties, sitting on the bridge together. Once, on this road, he had pulled me onto the yellow line that was supposed to separate the lanes of traffic, were there any traffic around here. But there wasn't. It had been raining then, and he, being romantic, had told me that he had always wanted to be able to say that he had kissed someone, in the middle of the road, and in the rain, and that now he could. I thought he might remember that and choose to sit beside me.

I didn't know what he was thinking, but he did sit down beside me. I saw that he really had pinned quite a few hopes on this day going well, that he too had suffered, and that he couldn't allow this night to end without my allowing it to happen, somehow being the deciding factor. But I didn't know how to do that for him. Instead, I took the pen out of my pocket and aimed for his eyeball. This time, things went better for me.

When I pictured what would happen when the pen went in his eye socket, I thought it would be much louder. I thought that surely, some deafening wail of pain and realization would emerge from him and that he would surely wake some neighbours, the ones with the watchful eyes, and I mentally took stock of all of their possible lines of sight to where we were, hidden not well by the iron railing on the bridge on one side, but better by the concrete barrier on the other. But all that came out of him was an odd gulp, like he was trying to get the pen out of his eye socket by breathing in too fast and inflating his head, such that it would become an inhospitable environment to pens, like when a balloon fought back against an impending pop by increasing a resistance force on whatever sharp implement it was that threatened its existence, before it finally gave in and exploded. But he was not a balloon. I reflected on that thought for a second and laughed a little. What an odd thing to think, I thought; *he was not a balloon!* It almost made me feel badly for him.

I had to act quickly; he could still see through the one eye. While he was stunned, I grabbed him by his balloon head and started rocking him back and forth into the iron railing. That didn't work well enough, I thought, so I dragged him by the same head about a foot towards the middle of the bridge and tried it with the concrete. It worked a little better, and I could see blood in his hair; it got in his good eye and made his grabbing at me practically futile. I could go on like this, I thought, or I could not. So I opted to not. I gave him a hard shove and pulled his legs out from underneath, one by one, until he was lying face down on the sidewalk. Once, a bunch of years ago, someone at a party had taught me how to hold an arm so that the person whose arm it was felt such a strain that the rest of their body went limp in a valiant attempt to save that one arm. The body was stupid. I did that to him now, and there was the scream I had wanted. He was trying to hold his face off of the sidewalk, kind of sideways so that the free end of the pen wouldn't hit anything and do any more damage. It would. I grabbed it and tried to rotate it like I was turning a crank, a kind of angled crank that would stir the inside of his head, but he just kept screaming.

This was taking way too long, and I could feel many other places where the bruises would come up. He kept trying for my face, but he couldn't seem to put much force into his movements anymore. I looked desperately around for something to do next.

The riverbank. The river was banked by large rocks that would come in rather handy in my current predicament. I didn't know if I could make it down to the riverbank and back and what he would get away with in the meantime, but it seemed my options were either to go get one of those rocks or to continue beating his head all day, and I went for it.

By the time I found a good one he was almost to the door of the house. He could still move quite quickly, it turned out. I grabbed a secondary rock, for the first one was too good to throw, and it flew toward him as if guided by Zeus himself. The fact that it knocked him down so cleanly was a sign that all of this was meant to happen, I thought. All of the difficulties I had encountered so far were just for suspense.

With my favourite rock, I found him, weeping it seemed, and I thought at first he was faking it, to make me feel badly for him. He had done it before. I took the rock and hit him a few times, until the shape of his head started to change, and I thought there was no way he could stay alive in that misshapen head, and so I stopped. I took his two arms and started to drag. It turned out that two arms were hard to hold onto. They were slippery, so I focused on one arm as my point of contact and kept dragging. He was going in the river.

TWO

They found a body in the river.

THEY HAVEN'T RELEASED the identity, but they confirmed that it was a male. So what. There are lots of males. I wondered if even that identification didn't prevent the body from self-identifying with whichever gender it would so choose. Perhaps it's all right to stifle the dead.

The radio didn't have anything else to say, but I continued listening. There was so much time to fill between here and there. Driving was one of the things I hated doing, just for the fact that it wasn't stimulating enough. Driving was like running or sitting alone without the television. It didn't take all that long for the world to subside. But it was only twenty minutes.

It was one of those things that just spiraled completely out of control. One minute, I was shopping for a sweater and the next, it was out of stock in my size but sure, they could call around. I didn't like the sweater all that much, but the clerk seemed so invested in it that of course, she could call around. I was in luck, though, they had one at another location only twenty minutes away. I didn't like the sweater all that much, but it was relatively cheap and would probably come in handy and now, they were expecting me. I hated when people imagined that other people weren't people. You didn't have to have worked in retail to know what it would be like for someone to call and say they were coming, for you to do something very specific in order to prepare for their arrival (in this case, setting aside a particular sweater), and then for that person not to show up.

There was literally a person only twenty minutes away who was actually spending time locating this sweater that, according to the mindset of someone who literally spent all day moving sweaters around, was a very special sweater indeed and had an intended owner who cared so much about it that she actually had the clerk at another store call around to the neighbouring locations (who knows how many she called before this one) in order to locate this one particular sweater that need only be set aside until its intended owner arrived. It would probably sit behind the counter, on display to anyone who happened to be making their own purchases.

They might look at the sweater and think, *that's an awfully nice sweater*, and might ask the nearby cashier about it. *No*, the cashier would say. That sweater is being held for someone driving in from out of town, the cashier would say, and the customer would compare the effort of the person driving for the sweater to their own effort in simply asking about the sweater and come to the conclusion that I, I who drove for the sweater, was infinitely more deserving of the very special sweater that already had an intended owner who not only demanded that a clerk call around to find it but who was actually *at this moment* driving in from out of town to get it. No one could ever suspect that I didn't like the sweater all that much.

I was supposed to meet someone. I would have to call, or text, or whatever. *I'll be a little late. I'm driving out of town to get a sweater. Full story later.*

When I was all caught up in making plans for the sweater acquisition, I hadn't managed to inform the clerk that I should not bother to call this particular location, because I didn't want to go there. Of course I *could* go there. I met all of the necessary conditions for going there—able-bodied, vehicle-owning, had sweater money to spend, etc., but I did not want to go there and if I had told the clerk, she might have taken it as an underhanded way of getting out of buying the sweater, into which this clerk had already put so much effort to locate.

It's just that physical spaces are capable of containing temporally distant things. The concept isn't really that unfamiliar, I thought. The past exists in spaces conducive to its persistence. That's just how things work. Every time I went home I remembered and felt it. It was past and present both, but only where it could stay alive—the strange house on Earl St.

There was nothing strange about the house, and I didn't ever think there was. I didn't know about its reputation until after I had met him; I had seen the house before its reputation, and there didn't seem to be anything whatsoever wrong with it. There were three bedrooms upstairs where he seemed to live, one more than the others. The other two rooms were guest rooms, according to his parents, but he had brought me into all of them at some point. They were in a separate section of the house downstairs, well, one of them. The other one wasn't technically his parent. It was the house on Earl St. where the crazy woman had stabbed herself.

I heard the story first from him. He found her when he came home from school. He was traumatized when, as a child, he had gone into the house after school only to find someone had broken in and stabbed and raped his mother. She was still alive. That's what she told him. Someone broke into the room where he now slept and had raped and stabbed his mother ten times when he was ten years old, once for each year. On the other hand, the strange house on Earl St. was where that crazy woman lived who had stabbed herself. It was especially abhorrent, given that she had a young son at home, a son who continued to live there, for whom she was supposed to care.

I would borrow cigarettes from his mother. He said that his mother didn't care what he did as long as he was safe about it; she knew everything. Once, she had walked in on him with a girl, naked, and later mentioned nothing about it. Anything we did would be fine; his mother would be fine. He could kiss me and touch me, and his mother would be fine. He would take one hand and put it above my head, and then the other. Then taking both of my wrists in one of his hands, he would reach to undo my pants and with his knees on my thighs there was not much I could do at that point except be fine. I would be fine because he was just getting comfortable; it would only take a minute; he only wanted to be inside of me because he loved me and I would be fine. It wasn't his fault about his mother. That was a terrible story.

Every so often when I had time to think about it, all of those years back, I would try to find out if he was dead. I would search him, variations of his name, he might have gone by his father's at some point, sometimes his mother's, but nothing ever came up. I thought if he were dead that at least an obituary, but nothing. There was a painter with the same name, and some graduate student who was going through the paces of finding himself in the usual ways, but nothing to confirm whether he himself was dead or alive. The closest doppelgänger was the graduate student, and sometimes I thought that by checking on his progress I could infer by analogy something pertinent about him, but of course this was false.

I couldn't confirm he was dead. I also couldn't confirm that he was alive. Someone who stayed alive would surely have left some kind of digital imprint in the decades since the internet, especially if, as he had emailed to me over a decade ago, he was starting medical school. Perhaps, though, he had committed some kind of crime that barred him from accessing the internet. If that were so, there would be a story about it. It was also possible that he had lived such a boring life since then that no one ever had any reason to remark on it. This was also possible. He could have done absolutely nothing, came of age, received government disability based on the years of psychiatric treatment he had undergone and was simply at home in a stupor on which no one ever remarked.

These were the kinds of things I thought when I had time to think them; for instance, when driving for twenty minutes to get something I didn't want from somewhere I didn't want to go while they talked about nothing on the radio.

I could go to his house. I had not even driven by in recent memory. When eventually I had left him, I still went by his house every now and then for a couple of years, since I had friends on the neighbouring streets. They were the ones who told me about the strange house on Earl St. But when they left for college I had had absolutely no reason to drive directly through that barely even a town when I could just as well go around. But I could go to his house. I was in the area, mobile, perfectly capable of going to any one of those houses. I could just drive by. So I did.

The house looked particularly unsatisfying. It was on part of the street that faced another perpendicular to it, so I turned down this perpendicular street, turned the car around, parked the car, and stared at this unsatisfying house. For the first few minutes I thought someone might come out. He might go check the mail or do some lawn work or something that would force him outside the house. But this idea was unreasonable, I came to believe. In any particular five-minute period, how likely someone would be to leave their house, was a low likelihood indeed. If I left my house a couple of times a day, and we took the surrounding five minute period as the period in which those leavings took place, then that constituted only ten minutes of a twenty four-hour day, which by six meant that the likelihood of him leaving the house then, if he were a two-time per day house leaver, at one in one hundred and forty four. I hadn't yet factored in the likelihood that he might arrive at the house, though. Counting the arrivals necessary to even out the departures, the odds were more like one in seventy-two.

The whole calculus was contrived, though. There was nothing to indicate that he even lived there, let alone that he left the house or arrived at it. I was only imagining him as he used to be—a skinny but broad-shouldered teenager with dark blond, close-cropped curly hair, dimples and bags around his eyes from not sleeping, who lived in the strange house on Earl St. and whose mother seemed very nice if a little inattentive. I could knock on the door.

Given how low the odds were that he actually lived there, I could very well knock on the door. It was likely that there was nobody home at all, but then I would never know if he did live there or not. If there were nobody home, I would go. If there were somebody home, I could go. But what if he did live there and was home?

The gun.

It was only a small thing, but I had imagined that one day, late at night, I would be stranded on the side of the road. A tire would go, or something, and someone would try something, and if they did, I had the gun. But I didn't know what to do with it. That's not to say I didn't know how to work it; I'd been shooting guns with my father since I was a child. I just didn't know how to take it out of the car and bring it with me to the door. I couldn't tuck it into my pants like anyone did, because I had chosen a dress that day. It was rather poor planning, now that I thought about it.

So I put it in the inside pocket of my blazer. If I bent over, it would surely fall out and someone would lose an eye, and it was obvious even if you didn't know what I had in there that I had *something* in there, but it was the best I could think of, given that I was socialized to exist relatively pocket-free.

I would move the car closer. It would be devastating to have to walk all of that way up the street and across Earl to the door. There were too many things that could happen in the time it took to move physically from one place to another, and I cursed the physical existence that limited my placement in space to this arduous continuity with respect to motion. Subatomic particles didn't have to move continuously in space, so why did I? Was it because I was so much bigger than they were? Even the smallest of humans was confined to moving in continuous space, though. So I would move the car —switching the gears and turning around and playing with the switches, surely I could make it from this part of the street to the driveway. It would look so intentional, were I to drive up to the house as if I had meant to do it. I imagined I had business there, very important business to anyone who saw me drive up, anyone, at least, who had not seen me parked a short distance away for the past five minutes fiddling with my gun. Perhaps they would think I had the most important business. Perhaps I did. It was enough to get the car from one place to another.

Once I turned off the car in the driveway, I realized there was no going back. Well, no, I didn't. I was perfectly capable of turning the car back on and simply driving away, but I didn't want to. I wanted to go to the door, and I wanted to see him. I wanted to see him as he used to be, as the memory that still lived in the space, and I wanted to show him that I was better now, so much better. If he only knew me now instead of then he wouldn't have, and I wouldn't have to do it.

Often, when I would say something after a long silence, or think of something terrible that could happen but likely wouldn't, my heart would make a run for it. I could feel it and hear it, and it jumbled my words and sometimes made my face red, made me cry. I would get frustrated at how I couldn't express myself adequately to whatever it was I wanted, and I imagined how much worse my heart would make it. I resented its capacity to exist contrarily to my will. I was used to not feeling the body parts I could not control and when this happened, it flew in the face of everything familiar. I recalled the fact that it corresponded to a heightened perception that some would express metaphorically as the slowing of time. Time did not slow for me; I sped on one step after the next until I met the door before I was ready and my hand knocked on it.

Nothing happened. Nothing happened, so I tried again. Again nothing happened, so I put my face right up close to the window, where I couldn't see much because of the blackout curtain. That was something new. One of the worst things about the house was its solid placement in space and time. I would go in during the afternoon sometimes, go through some extended ordeal, and leave the same afternoon, while the house and everything around it pretended that nothing out of the ordinary occurred. I often thought that was why so many people failed to generalize particular occurrences into instances of some general kind, especially traumatic ones. Certainly, certain kinds of events would be so signifi-cant that something, anything, would change irrevo-cably, and yet there was the world, just sitting there, indifferent. *That* didn't happen. It *couldn't* have. Go home, get a call, go over, save him again, go home. I was fourteen and he was fifteen and nothing mattered.

When I had stepped two feet to the right to start walking around the house, the door opened and I looked at him. It was terrible. He seemed the same size, but he had lost some hair and was letting the rest grow out. I guessed that he figured that some long hair was better? It was misguided. The face, though, was just like the old one. The new face was the old one but rougher, somehow, not in the sense that he looked more haggard, like he had lived life hard and bore the look of it, but rougher just in texture, like he didn't care to wash it very often, and oily. It was the eyes, though, that were the most troublesome. They seemed to know me.

I froze. I was two feet from the door and he wasn't coming out, and I froze. It was what I always did. I figured that it was my body's way of avoiding criticism. Surely, someone who wasn't and couldn't do *anything at all* couldn't be blamed, couldn't be affected, couldn't be hurt. But it didn't matter, and this stupid body didn't recognize that. I could force it, though. I was capable of that. I imagined how other people sometimes said that guns made them feel powerful, and I thought that if I felt it in my pocket, I might feel that too and come up with a solution for this predicament I'd gotten myself in— the one where I was two feet from the door and he was there, knowing me.

I shot him in the face.

Seconds later I was in the car again, making deliberate movements. *Feet first*, I told myself, getting in. *Shut the door. Find the key. Turn it to start the car. Check your side mirror on the way to the blindspot. Look directly behind the car while backing up.* I checked to make sure that I still had everything I had and I did. It didn't leave the car, because I was relatively pocket-free, and I couldn't have brought it with me.

I thought it was an appropriate way to leave him. I knew that soon, I wouldn't know what had happened. I would look for an obituary or an announcement, and I might not believe it when I read it. My standard for accepting declarations as either one of true or false was well above where it might be, given how often I had seen these standards fall apart, change, or be refused in civil society. Still, I thought, it was better than nothing. For now, I would know.

And the world would continue. I was on my way to the store to get a sweater, and when I got there, the cashier might ask what had taken me so long to get from one place to another. There were any number of ways one might answer the question. I would be so focused on that sweater that no one could ever suspect that I had ever thought anything the entire twenty minutes' drive besides a repetition of that one all-consuming goal of the non-temporal ideal customer, who demanded special locating services and drove from one town to another thinking nothing other the entire time than *sweater sweater sweater.* I could be that for them. I decided that, although I hadn't thought about it at the time, the face really was the best place for a bullet. Perhaps it would seem cleaner to whomever would find him. I would get the sweater, I would meet my friend, and no one would ever notice the missing time, because I was there for all of it. I would smile and say nothing remarkable, and no one would remark on it.

THREE

SOMETHING WASN'T QUITE RIGHT. I didn't know it when I came in the door, but after a while, something wasn't quite right.

I couldn't figure out how it was that they got time to pass. It didn't seem to work the same way for me. When I was younger, I could go out to a restaurant and eat alone. I would bring a book, and everything would be all right until the food actually came. What does one think about while eating the food, though? Where does one look? That's when everything got in.

And then there was no book. I didn't know when I had stopped reading so much, but I figured it must have something to do with the fact that whenever I tried to read them, I couldn't think about them. It was not enough to stop my thinking so that I could just *think* along with the book. Every now and then I got to read them, but it was never like before. Perhaps the new books weren't good enough, I thought. But that couldn't be it. Certainly the quality of the books I read hadn't declined; the quality of the books couldn't be dependent upon when it was I chose to read them. That couldn't hold.

So I went into the restaurant, but I ordered takeout. And when I got the takeout, I would take it out, but I didn't have anywhere to go. If the parking lot was not busy or had a corner, I would eat it in the car. The problem was the smell. If the car smelled, they would know. I could eat with the windows open, but if the windows were open, I worried that would seem like an invitation. It would break the barrier from walled to not-walled, and then anyone might come up to me. No, it was better to keep the windows shut. I could open the windows while driving. If the windows were open while driving, that was fine. No one could misinterpret that. The problem was that there was nowhere I could go where they couldn't. Everyone had the same capabilities as I did.

I didn't think it was fair. The problem with the body was its visibility. The body itself was an invitation, as if to say look, there's a person here. I could often tell how I was feeling based on how I was noticed out in public. When I was particularly downtrodden, people would bump into me more frequently. I was certain that if I graphed it, the correlation would hold. I wondered what kind of metaphysical mechanism might be going on there. When things were good, people would naturally move as a flock around me. And when things were wrong, they would bump around like drunken children who hadn't yet gotten used to their physical form. There seemed to be a fluctuation of spatial self-awareness in others, but the fact that it corresponded to my disposition didn't make any sense unless I made the spatial argument—that my soul had gotten bigger or smaller. That didn't make any sense because spatiality was reserved for the material. It was body or nothing.

The back of his head seemed sad. I wondered at this too; what kind of perception is going on here such that the back of a person's head can seem sad. But it did. That much was certain. And I didn't think it was me this time. There was definitely something about the head itself that seemed more ashamed, like it shouldn't have to exist there and then, though it did. Any sort of correlation didn't seem to stick; the number of hairs, the colour, the shape of the head. It all didn't seem to work, even though all together, it did. There wasn't any way to account for the "all", though. The "all" was something else, and all of it.

The head sat calmly at the table with two women. The left one seemed particularly interested in the front of the head, while the right one didn't quite. I wondered how the right one had gotten there. It was probably promised that another back of the head would show up and then didn't. Or maybe it was supposed to have plans with the left one when this head showed up and ruined everything. The left one probably had some kind of pathological desire to please male heads that made it impossible to focus on the right one's pressing and complex issues, the ones that she had been hoping to talk to the left one about, if only this head hadn't come along. It would be one of the final straws for the left one. She didn't seem capable of treating the right one as the second self a true friend should be.

For a second I suspected it. For a moment I considered, and then I was as certain as the end of time. *It's him.* He should have been dead. I wished I had killed him then. No one would have blamed me. Or perhaps they would have, but they would have also attributed the action to my youth or my female fragility or my whatever it was they considered mitigating circumstances eighteen years ago before I felt I was allowed to exist. It was odd how that worked; when I saw the knives in his room, I didn't even consider using them. They were his knives; he used them. He used them on himself and he could use them on me, but there was no way I could use the knives. It would be like using someone else's hands. They just don't work like that. I would have had to have found some other way to kill him, but I should have.

I looked back at the left one and felt disgusted. She had no idea what the sad back of the head had done, would do. I tended to think that such horrible people wouldn't have the capacity to just go out, go into a restaurant, sit down, spend an hour there. I couldn't account for their time passing. It seemed that such evil should not be capable of persistence. If it wasn't, then where did it go when its bodies went to eat in restaurants? There was no way to account for it. I thought the left one might leave with the head, while the right one would have to find another way home. The left one had brought her there, or perhaps she and the head had, but they would not leave together. If they left together, then they would have to go to the same place, and the opportunity to lose the right one would be lost. There was some reason why the left one was interested in the head, and I knew the head was interested in the left one because she was interested in it. No matter how many times I was told that this was a rather reductive way of thinking of it, I never saw any evidence to the contrary. There weren't two contradictory premises here: that men were and were not interested in the easiest thing. There were two complementary ones: that men were interested in the easiest thing and also liked to think they weren't.

My food came—a sandwich that wouldn't fall apart when I ate it and that didn't require any utensils. You couldn't eat anything with utensils while the steering wheel was in the way, and you couldn't move to any other seat in the car—that would look odd. When things looked odd, someone would choose to investigate, and if someone chose to investigate, that would negate the whole purpose of being alone in the car in the first place; no one to look at, no one to look back, no one to look at me oddly when I explained that they were ruining it and that they shouldn't have looked in. I understood that I only had a few seconds to pay and then leave. If I stayed any longer, that would indicate that there was something to stay for. When there wasn't anything to stay for, any delay would look odd. I could claim to be waiting for something that eventually didn't come, but I didn't think I could pull it off. It was amazing how people understood temporality intuitively and yet not at all.

I did a quick check on the table in an attempt to see what stage of the meal these three had reached. I couldn't see any dishes; that was inconclusive. They could not have arrived, or they could have already left. There weren't any linens; they could have not arrived, or they could have already left. There were coffee cups; either they were all tired, or this was an after dinner coffee. It's possible that one person decided to defy convention and order coffee at the beginning of the meal, and that the others jumped on the bandwagon. It was more likely that the meal was finished and that I didn't have long.

So I took the sandwich to the car to wait. I couldn't see the door from where I had parked, by design, so I had to move the car. I didn't think anyone would notice that. They would have had to have been staring at me the entire time I moved the car. If, on the other hand, they weren't, then all they would see is one car leaving a parking spot and another parking in a parking spot. I figured that it wasn't likely someone was staring at me for that long, so it would be all right. I considered briefly that even if they did, they could go fuck themselves, because I didn't have to justify moving my fucking car if I didn't want to.

It was taking an extraordinarily long time to finish the coffee. Something was amiss. The left one was not going with the head. The right one had prevailed. Nothing was going to happen. I had made the terrible mistake I always did in assuming that he would be successful—that he could have whatever he wanted. It wasn't like that. Other people didn't have to give in to him. The left one probably had gotten bored, or she could tell something was off about him, but she didn't know what, and she was working on worming her way out of the situation using the right one and all of her pressing and complex issues as some kind of trivial excuse for the fact that she didn't want his cock jammed into her. He would see right through it.

I decided to eat the sandwich. It would make the car smell, and he would notice when he got into it, but it was going to smell anyway if I left the sandwich in it and didn't eat it. My car already smelled. I was going to have to deal with that; it would smell like the back of his head looked. I was just a sad woman with a smelly car who's been waiting too long in the parking lot, and I hated him for thinking it. I would just have to deal with that.

And what did you do last night? I imagined someone asking—no one, not anyone. *I ate a sandwich and killed a man*, I said. I burst out laughing at the idea. Now I was the sad woman in a smelly car who was laughing to myself. I remembered how he had used that against me. I would never know, he said, whether my art was really brilliant, or just the ravings of some madwoman who had inherited it from my crazy mother. The former meant I could take the credit, I guessed. The latter meant I could not. It would be my work but not, the work of a disease, not a disease embodied in a woman but a free-floating one, that could create art and could be blamed for things and one that used my physical form but somehow wasn't it. The disease was nearby but not in me, or in me but not of me, or of me but not me and never could I take credit or blame for what it did.

The women left. The women left together and left him there. They had made a better decision than I had, but I didn't think they had done it on purpose, so I didn't think they had anything on me. And he just sat there. Why was it all right for him to just sit there, when I couldn't? He could sit there, drinking a coffee, doing what? What was he thinking about? Did it take him that long to process that he had to actually sit there and drink coffee and allow what had happened to happen again thoughtfully and over the course of so many minutes? It didn't seem natural to me. It didn't work. If I had tried that, they would know. They would know the difference, and I would look odd, while he just sat there, the most natural thing in the world, drinking his fucking coffee like he hadn't fucking ruined me.

I would use it. I would use it to get him in the car. He was definitely expecting something to happen with the left one, and now that it hadn't, all women were responsible. I would use it to get him in the car. Getting out of my head for a moment, I figured that were he to come out of the restaurant right now and be offered a ride in a car with a woman, he would take it as the most natural thing in the world. It wasn't that one woman had left and another had arrived; they were all the same woman to him. For a moment things were looking down, and now they were looking up again. There was a woman who wasn't interested and then who was. Fuck the left woman, I thought. He couldn't. Fuck me, then? No. I knew I wasn't the left woman.

Get in the car, I willed. I thought that he might just come over to my car and get in. That would be the most natural thing to do. But of course he didn't. I would have to *do something*. I turned on the car; it smelled like a sandwich. I turned on the vent with the air freshener clip on it, and the smell of fresh laundry mingled with onions and tomato sauce. It would have to do. I marveled at what kind of disgusting things men were willing to put up with to have their cocks rubbed, the kind of things that would totally negate the idea for me. I felt disgusting. I didn't even know if he would get in the car. But of course I did. I had to loop around the lot to get angled in the right direction. I couldn't picture him having to walk across the car to get in it; I would have to drive up to him with the door he was to get in facing him. That would make it the easiest.

But he kept moving. By the time I got back around to him, he was halfway across the drive, walking towards his own car. I couldn't let him get to it though, and so I got a little too close. I didn't want to scare him, just get his attention, just enough for him to know that he could be scared. I got a little too close, and he turned toward me. I thought he would be angry, but then I remembered that he would be hopeful, just coming off a loss. I stopped the car and waved at him. "Hello!" I yelled.

Then I remembered that people couldn't generally hear me when I spoke to them from inside my car. I had to roll down the window. "Hello!" I yelled, as if I hadn't before.

"Hello!" he mimicked.

"Can you fly?" I asked.

He looked at me oddly. It was what he had asked me the first time we had met. I was repeating the conversation line by line, but he didn't catch on. He just looked at me oddly. I thought of everyone who had covered up a misspoken sentence by repeating something with similar phonetics, but I couldn't think of anything and the moment lasted too long. He had to start to move again, and I couldn't let him.

"Are you OK?" I asked, as if I didn't know whether I had hit him or not.

That was completely understandable, apparently. "Yes, I'm fine," he said and smiled. I was right.

"Perhaps you'd like to get a coffee," I somewhat asked, aware of the fact that he had already drunk quite a bit. I was therefore certain that he liked it and could not awkwardly respond that he didn't in a mistaken display of honesty when he should have been playing strategically. He could have drunk too much coffee already, I supposed, but he wouldn't think to say that. People don't think to say that.

"Sure," he said. "You owe me one after that near miss."

It was not a near miss, I thought. He was just trying to make me feel obligated to him. He didn't have to think about that one very long; it must be habitual for him to be a fucking asshole. People don't think to say things like that unless they're that way.

"Get in," I told him. Then he looked a little odd. Could he see what I was doing? Yes. Yes, he could. Did he believe that he saw it? No. So he would get in the car. The second order was much more important than the first.

When he got in the car, I wasn't quite sure what to do. I had a plan for when the car stopped again, but it was the *in between* that was the real problem. What did people say when they were driving in cars from place to place? What did they talk about? Whatever it was, it would certainly seem to be whatever was the most important thing. If there were only five minutes to talk, then whatever came out should be the most important thing, whatever it was that best summarized everything and anything and would be what I remembered from now on about riding in the car for five minutes.

I didn't have to say anything. I was just all women. It didn't actually matter to him.

He talked about the restaurant they were seemingly both in, and he neglected to mention that he was there with anyone. He kept saying "I", as if "he" was there alone and just happened to meet someone else who was there alone, as if they had never existed, as if the left one especially had never existed. I tried not to let on that I knew differently, that I had watched and seen and knew differently. He was happy with the occasional nod of *go on*. I thought maybe it looked as if I were focused too hard on my driving, and the thought made me focus too hard on my driving. And so I pretended to be focusing on my driving by making a point of doing it, in order to avoid having to answer anything he said.

"Here we are," I said and pulled up to a park.

"Where?" he inquired.

"As if you don't fucking know," I said.

"I don't understand."

"We met here eighteen years ago."

He didn't say anything that time. Perhaps he hadn't looked at me yet; perhaps it didn't matter. He couldn't have forgotten. Had I changed so much since then that he actually couldn't recognize me, that his perception didn't form the connection between a prior physical form and this one? That could happen, perhaps, if I had no face. The faces always stayed the same. Did I have no face? What was wrong with him? "Get out of the car," I told him. "I want to take a walk by the river."

And he didn't care. He didn't care that I swore at him fifteen seconds ago, and he didn't care that I said I was taking him out for coffee and then didn't. He got out of the car.

I tried to focus on my walking in order not to have to speak to him, but that didn't work. I stared at the ground, and I thought that came off as some kind of self-deprecation. Poor so-and-so, always looking down. Chin up, he'd say, and save me from all of that. That was how it worked; those with higher chins thought they were better people.

"I want to tell you about a woman I used to be,"

I started. He looked at me oddly. "No I don't," I added.

"What's wrong, -------?"

He used my name.

"What's wrong? Everything's wrong! Everything's been wrong for so long now, and I don't think you get it."

"It'll be all right now," he said. "It's all going to be all right," he said, as if he were the smartest fucking person to have thought of such a thing to say. I couldn't stand the fact that he had a mouth and used it to say such inane and stupid things. I couldn't stand that he could inhale the air that allowed him to do so.

I had to take it.

"What?"

"Take the air."

"I don't understand."

"You don't need to."

I put my face on his and tried to suck the air out of his lungs. He wouldn't keep his mouth still and kept breathing through his nose. This wasn't going to work. He just thought I was kissing him and was very bad at it. What a fucking moron. I tried to keep doing it while I thought of something better. I thought maybe for a second I could lovingly grasp him by the neck and then just hold on, but his forearms seemed stronger than mine, and I would have to debilitate those if I was going to get anywhere. If I were busy debilitating his forearms, then I couldn't hold his neck. I thought about clotheslining him on a tree branch, something conveniently neck height I could push him into, but I couldn't look around from behind his face. Then I figured it out.

I pushed him onto the ground as if I wanted to

step it up a notch, and he went down willingly. Then all I had to do was angle the arms properly, which required flipping him onto his stomach. He wouldn't go for that naturally, so I would have to do it by force. I tried grabbing at his hand to try to twist it around his back, but the angles didn't work. I didn't understand how the angles were supposed to work and how I used to do this, to disable a man, by disabling the arm, which you could do by twisting it around the back and up. Maybe women were raped because the angles weren't right.

But he still had hope. All I had to do was use that.

"Turn over," I said. And he did. And that was that.

I put my knee into his back to hold him down. I put my left hand on his head to keep that from moving. The head is where bodily space lives. I covered up the sadness on the back of his head and kept it from getting up, kept it from moving. With my right hand I grabbed the blade from my pocket. It wasn't a switchblade; that was illegal. It just had a little knob on the blade that you could push on so that you could still open it with one hand. If it was loose enough, you could flick it open, but I hadn't been able to do that since I started using the blade to cut apples.

What do you need a knife like that for? Someone had asked. I had bought it in a shop I had wandered into while waiting for somebody else, and thought I had managed to buy it without anyone seeing, but when I came back out someone had asked, *what do you need a knife like that for?* And I had responded: to cut apples. And I did.

Now I was considering where best to cut off the

air supply. If I went for the torso, the air could still circulate, and I wanted to cut it off. I couldn't cut it off at the source of the air, though, because the source of the air is nothing but holes, and you can't cut holes. They're immaterial, and only material things can be cut. *Holes are the spatial immaterial.* They're atomistic, uncuttable, spatial immaterials.

I went for the in between. In between the source of the air and its destination was a flexible tube that turned a hole into a bag, and I went for that. I aimed for the inner hole, and I hoped that I could mangle its periphery enough that the hole ceased to exist; a full hole is not a hole. A hole filled with blood is not a hole, it's blood. Blood is what it is and if it's in the hole there is no hole there's only blood.

FOUR

EVERY SINGLE ONE of them was not me, or I was
them, or they weren't. Perhaps it didn't matter. My
mother always said that it didn't matter. Sex and love
were two different things, and they didn't necessarily
go together, or they weren't together, or they repelled
each other. I thought maybe the last one. It seemed
that way. Perhaps it was real for other people, or
perhaps it was made up as part of everything else
that was made up to make me feel like less of a
person than I was supposed to be. I thought maybe
that one.

It took him three days to tell me that he loved
me. Day one we met. Day two I didn't remember.
Day three I didn't know. Day four, he'd never felt like
this before and if I only felt it too he could die happy.
But he wouldn't. He flat out refused. It was like he
didn't care about me at all. I didn't know I could
distrust other people's judgments, though. You can't
tell other people how to feel, they told me. But then I
always had to feel as I was told, and it didn't make
sense. In any case, I believed him because I'd always

been told that people knew themselves best, and that you couldn't question their judgments about their own feelings.

There were a couple of assumptions you had to make, though: (1) that they were honest. If they were just lying about their feelings, then there was nothing to trust. It wasn't a two-step process where they felt something and then noted that feeling and then reported it with the intention of stating what they believed to be accurate. (2) That they knew what they were talking about. If you don't know what you're talking about, then you can honestly believe you feel a way even if that way does not exist and you're making it up in order to make me feel like less of a person. Everyone else got to feel, and I had to guess how I was supposed to.

I was very good at it.

There were three days between day one and day four, and he took that as evidence of the strength of the feeling. It was equally possible, I later thought, that it was just as much evidence for the fact that he didn't know what he was talking about. Consider this analogy: If someone believed that they were born, grew up, and died in a matter of days, you would think that they were lying, they didn't know what they were talking about, or there was something terribly wrong with them. The fact of the matter was (3). There was something terribly wrong with him. He didn't believe what he should have believed, and I believed all of it when I shouldn't have.

This is how you start categorizing things to believe or not to believe: when he said that he loved me after three days, it should not have been believed. To believe it would necessitate that something was necessarily *good*, and there's no such thing as a necessary good. But there's so much pressure to believe the good. No one, on the other hand, ever questions it when someone tells them that they're cheating; that they fucked someone else. Terrible things are honest. Terrible things are real.

After seven days he left. His parents sent him to Christian camp and after a month he came back with a bunch of new Christian rock albums. And he had fucked someone else when he said he wouldn't. He called me before he came back, just to let me know. He wanted to be honest. He didn't want me to think that he would lie about something like that. That would make him a terrible person, and he didn't want that. I decided that he would want me to feel fine about that. Sex and love were two different things, and I would be the woman who believed that. That would make him happy, I thought, if I believed that.

Before me, there was Christa, and he only dated Christa because he knew that she would fuck him if he waited it out. After Christa there was Melanie, and I didn't know what happened between him and Melanie. I couldn't imagine them having spent any time together at all, not a moment. She was too stupid. Then there was me. There might have been Katelynn, whom he was with when I met him, but there wasn't. I eventually recognized that pattern; there was a woman when we met, and then there wasn't anymore. I wondered what happened to the discarded women; it had never happened to me. They seemed so old when you called them women, but to call them girls made me feel like less of a person.

Then there was the girl from camp. Then there was the girl at the hospital. Then there was Amanda and Melissa. Melissa was the odd one out; she threatened to kick him down the stairs if he tried to touch her below the waist. He saw her anyway. I thought Melissa must have been magic. He told me that his friends thought Melissa was prettier than I was, and the idea was that that would explain it. Amanda was really nice; we became good friends. For a while we could tell each other stories about our mutual boyfriend, and it didn't seem all that odd. I thought Amanda had better stories, though. Once, she serenaded him, she said. It was a goodbye thing, Amanda assured me. That was fine, I guessed.

He told me that I should try dating his friend. He knew I liked tall men, he said, and he had a tall friend. He brought us both over to his house at the same time, and it was true that he was tall, but it just didn't seem to fit him—like he was too tall for himself or something. He would probably have to duck through a custom made doorway, I thought and laughed.

I had to keep the list ready, just in case. Someday, he would try to tell me that he loved me again, and I would have to have my list ready. But it was nothing to think about.

I lay awake in bed again, just like I always did, unless I remembered to buy something to make all of that go away. It was easier to handle unconscious, I thought. It was another way for the body to enslave me—to keep me awake and stuck in it while it recycled old and tired thoughts. When I thought those thoughts, I felt as young as I had then, and then a sense of incongruence between what I thought and what I knew myself to be, and then I felt like the two times might become simultaneous somehow. I would be lying in bed and just thinking but also repulsed because he might use my thinking to transport himself here, not in space, but in time, even though I thought he might be dead by now. I didn't think that would stop him, though. I've learned not to trust the rules of the physical universe, and I remembered how he laughed at that too, as if there were some good reason to doubt it besides being a bastard. (Not to poke fun at bastards, though; that's an old habit that would also probably be dead by now, poking fun at bastards. I certainly didn't want to get caught in past times.)

Here's another incongruence: everybody thinks that time moves only forward, that you can't change the past, and everyone also despises that fact and attempts to defy it at every opportunity. Of course you can't change the past, and for that reason, time is an irredeemable bastard. The product of a bastard reason, someone said, I couldn't remember who. I wondered who might be the legitimate parents of reason, and how at least I had never gotten pregnant. There was always a pile of condoms in the garbage can, not all of them were mine. They were all sorts of colours, because colours appealed to teenagers, I guess, and they just left them around the school as if to promote safe sex, and I guessed they did, in some cases. In other cases, they prevented bastards—some but not others.

If I wasn't going to sleep that night, I might as well get up, I thought. The thought was more difficult than I anticipated, though, because I thought that because I was awake I could get up. That turned out not to be the case. The body is so tired, sometimes, and it doesn't do what it wants, because he won't let it or I won't let it, or it wasn't supposed to. I couldn't quite reason it out, but it happened anyway.

That's how it worked. I didn't want to open my eyes, though, because there were always things in the dark. They didn't take hold until they were seen, but they were there. They were blank bits of darkness just waiting to take form, and once you saw them you could feel them. If I could keep my eyes closed, they wouldn't come, but I didn't. It was because I thought about standing up that it happened, but I couldn't stand and now they were there—the bastards of human perception, too used to putting forms to things not to do it when there wasn't anything to form.

I tried to make the dark of the corner into him— a skinny but broad-shouldered teenager with dark blond, close-cropped curly hair, dimples and bags around his eyes from not sleeping. I wanted too much colour, though, and I overstepped. A form appeared, but not the one I wanted; it was almost the same but there could be no face, no hair, nothing definite. I wondered what was so terrifying about the non-specific human form, the human that could not be identified as *that particular* human, and why it appeared now.

Or maybe it was him, making his way across time. He had become a super genius physicist who had figured out time travel and come forward from the past to see me, tracing me by my thoughts. But that didn't make sense. If he were in the past, then he wouldn't have *become* anything. He would have figured out time travel, and I would have been there to see, since I was there. So he wasn't coming from the distant past. If it was from the near past, then I didn't know why he would bother coming to the future when he could have just found me and called me and had a lovely chat, instead of becoming a non-particular human in the corner of my bedroom. So he wasn't from the near past. And in the future, he was dead. The only possible conclusion was that I was trying too hard to make two times into one; there was only one thing and it was the present, and no specific man was in the corner.

But there wasn't. Every time I looked directly at him, he wasn't there.

I got up and left the room, tired of this nonsense. I would be tired somewhere else, I thought. I went downstairs and opened the fridge. If I drank anything, I would have to pee again before I slept, so I didn't want to do that. But I was thirsty. If I could fall asleep, I would forget I was thirsty, but I couldn't sleep, so I might as well drink something, even if drinking something meant I couldn't sleep.

When I turned around, he was there again. I could tell it was the same one, even though he didn't have a face, because there couldn't be that many non-particular men around the house. In any case, I could tell it was the same one. It felt like the same one. But if he was a non-particular, how could there be any number of particulars of him? That's what didn't make sense. I thought about it in his face while he stood there, just nothing, nothing at me. The world was different when there was no light to make people honest; that was as literally as I could say it. It was dark out, and because of that, I couldn't see what he wanted. Of course, I never could, but during the daytime at least it was more. They called darkness a cover, but it wasn't so much. It was some-thing else entirely; it was the freedom from that oppressive lightness that made everything seem as it was. Everything as it was was disappointing. I remembered thinking, when I was younger, that *if*

44

only, then *something*, just in general. If only this, then I wouldn't have to deal with that. But the more I saw of the world, the more disappointing it was. Distant places were the same; distant people were the same. At least when you couldn't see them, you could imagine them, and when it was dark, you couldn't see him.

I didn't think I was imagining him, though. He moved with me; imaginations don't move. They are the static form of movement, the image, the thing as it was plastered onto something else, ridding it of all dimensionality. In some cases, that was a good thing, I thought. Pictures were prettier than people. He was a better image than a man.

I wanted to go out and check on him, but it didn't feel right. It was dark, but outside, still someone might be there. I wouldn't have the walls keeping them out. They could be there and wonder what I was up to. He was only out back, though, and sometimes I did go to see him. During the day, when they left for work, I could tell I was alone for as far as I could see, and I would go out to visit him. I didn't understand how people could be surprised to find that there was someone in their near proximity when it was so obvious when people were nearby, but then I negated that thought immediately because of that one time. One time, someone had snuck up on me. So it wasn't true in all cases and therefore couldn't be counted on.

That was another thing entirely. I remembered that time I was surprised, and how for hours afterward my colleague told the story about how he had snuck up on me and how I had jumped. I wanted to tell everyone, I had only done it for his sake. I thought that maybe there was some kind of lag between what I thought, what I felt, and what I said, and what I did. Other people seemed to just go around feeling and saying things, but I always said what I was supposed to and when I was supposed to be surprised, I made a point to jump. I had to, I thought. It made other people feel better, like I was alive, just like them. It didn't come naturally, though, so I wondered how I had gotten stuck in this partic- ular form when I felt I had much more in common with the shadow in the kitchen.

I sat down on the couch, and he just stood there. I thought he had turned around from the fridge, because I could feel him looking in my direction, even though he had nothing to look with. He was *something*, and definitely *at* me. I'd better go to check on him, I thought. I was just being silly.

In the backyard, under the single tree that grew in the centre of the yard, the one that was supposed to have ruined it for doing anything useful in, like building a pool or a patio or whatever people did, there he was. At least, I assumed he was there. I had put him there, and he hadn't moved since. I made him into an image, I thought. Except this image was not perfected by the process; it stayed there, constantly degrading, somehow becoming more human as it disintegrated. I thought that might be what humans were, after all. What was human about them was the capacity to disintegrate, and whatever it was that defied temporality was something else, whatever it was that kept me awake even though I could feel my body's hatred for it. That was a human thing too, to live in hateful little bodies that, in the end, were just squishy flesh buckets held together by will.

Some of the time, I could tell the difference.

When I felt there was someone outside, sometimes it was actually just him, and sometimes, there was someone actually there. This time, it was just him— well, the both of us, I thought. The nothing man stood in the window, looking at me as part of the reflection of the glass, the part that wasn't there.

When I had put him there, under the tree, originally, I thought that it would be obvious. Anyone who knew anything about how dirt worked would know. They would be able to see it. I kept reminding myself that I didn't *have* to be honest with them, and that if I weren't, they wouldn't be able to tell. They wouldn't be able to tell like I wasn't able to tell when he was being dishonest with *me*, and I had learned. There might have been something terribly wrong with me, but he was one thing, no particular thing less. I thought that if someone were to look outside, they'd be able to sense the hollowness of the ground. *They didn't.* I thought that if I pulled the dirt away to check to make sure he was still there, they would notice the ground disturbed. *They didn't.* I thought that the smell would come out and whoever was in the area would recognize it unmistakably as the scent of disintegrating human flesh buckets, but *they didn't.* So he stayed there. Day one, day two, day three, day four, and so on until I didn't really *lose* count but more made a point of not counting. Perhaps they could only tell if I counted, I thought.

It was childish to take a man and put him under a tree. I felt I was giving in to my younger self when I did it, and that I might become her again if I did, and then I went ahead with it anyway. That sneaky bastard would always be behind me, and it didn't matter if he were there too. After a while, though, I regretted it. It was like when I lied and told him that

I loved him too. I thought if I did it, then *something*. I didn't want to grow old with him, and I didn't want to grow old with him under the tree either. I just didn't want him there, but he always somehow was.

I couldn't get him out through the house. That would get all over the carpets and wreck everything. I also couldn't bring him around the side; he might hit something that would be damaged, and he would probably disintegrate all over whatever it was. You couldn't trust him not to. I couldn't leave him there; he would be there longer than I was, messing up the whole yard. It wasn't the tree that was the problem, I wanted to go back in time and tell the real estate agent. It was the man under the tree who wouldn't move.

And so I waited. Even though something had to happen, it never did. And even when I was supposed to sleep through it, I didn't. And whenever I went out back, there was nobody there to say *Ha! There's a man in the yard, I knew it!* And I would finally be honest about it and admit that yes, the past existed and here it was in the yard, just lying around disintegrating. *That* would be the moment I would become an image, I thought. That was when time would freeze and I wouldn't have to go along with it anymore, just stop and not do it and fuck all those bastards.

It was no use waiting here for it, though. Nothing seemed to be happening, and everyone was already in bed. I could feel it. So I went back inside. I thought about drinking something again and how it would make me have to pee, and I did it anyway, because I was thirsty. I found the last pill that I thought I could hide from myself, as if I would one day forget it and then, at some point in the future, remember it in a great time of need. I never forgot it, though, so the plan never worked. I took it and stared at the non-particular man in the living room, who was too good for a face, and when I started to feel heavy I climbed back up the stairs while he followed behind. Back in bed, I closed my eyes and he disappeared.

FIVE

NO ONE HAD EXACTLY INVITED me to the party, but I was there, and I knew that I had better act like I belonged there, or else people would think I didn't. Lizzie's house, they said. There's a party at Lizzie's house later, you should come. Yeah, that would be great, I said. They didn't give me the address, though. That didn't matter, I thought, because I knew the address. So I went to the address that I knew and decided not to consider that perhaps they didn't give me the address because they didn't really want me to come. But then why ask? To be polite, some might say. How is it polite to invite someone somewhere you don't want them to be and then make them uncomfortable when they get there? I wanted to know. It just didn't seem polite, but I was there, and I couldn't do anything now, because anything would look weird.

They all seemed so young, I thought. I knew that I had grown up in a different kind of place with a different kind of people. I imagined that all house parties in high school would be like ones in the movies. Fuck, I forgot that they didn't even call it high school. That was also a movie thing. It was secondary school. I went to secondary school. It had been three years since I'd seen him last, and I was at Lizzie's house.

Lizzie was a legend. Nobody knew it, but he had told me all about it and then repeatedly after. He thought I would understand, he said, that he would never love me as much as Lizzie, because I wasn't as good as Lizzie. In the eighth grade, Lizzie went down the water slide and her breast popped out of her bikini top. I tried to imagine Lizzie in a bikini but then couldn't, because I was more attractive than Lizzie and wouldn't wear a bikini myself. Therefore, it was impossible that Lizzie should have ever worn one. I secretly thought that despite all measure, despite all consistent measure between me and the others, that they had somehow found a way to be more attractive. Lizzie could be more attractive than I was even though Lizzie had a pot belly, she was short, and she had a mole on her face that for the love of God why didn't someone have it checked out already. The last time he broke down, he said, it was the greatest feeling. There was nothing left to lose. That's when he asked out Lizzie, and she said no. That was the Lizzie-legend. I would never live up to Lizzie, because Lizzie didn't really exist.

She didn't exist except for the look on her face when I came to the door and she didn't expect me to be there. Someone had invited me, they said, they guessed. I imagined the movie party where nobody knew whose house it was, you got to meet people you would never talk to during the day, and at the end of the evening, everyone would finally come to under-stand each other. Except that wasn't the case—I had shown up half-invited, and the only people there were people with that look on their face. Lizzie's mother ran the water filtration plant and Lizzie was in the artsy crowd—the one that didn't actually produce any art but dressed funny and dyed their hair sometimes. They smoked a lot of weed and talked about nothing, just reveling in their own self-importance. I thought that on a global scale, Lizzie was not important. Lizzie would die like the rest of them, a flesh heap and then nothing, and nothing would exist of her to talk about. *Except for him.*

I honestly didn't know whether I would have preferred to be myself or Lizzie. Lizzie had no benefits to speak of from this unexpected and uninvited adulation, and while neither did I, she at least knew something of it. All the time that he was talking about Lizzie, he was *with me.* That didn't mean to be anything significant; it was just a necessary condition of the fact that I knew anything about Lizzie at all. He had told me. That was that.

So I took off my shoes while Lizzie stood impatiently. She seemed not to want to offer me anything, as even though everyone else in the room had a cup for the keg, I had to ask for one. I wondered if it was more rude to ask for one or to go without one, which would make me stand out more. Didn't anyone show up for parties slightly late? I had shown up slightly late, in order not to be the first there. I also didn't want to miss anything, so only slightly late. Still, there weren't enough eyes on me to make them seem non-threatening. All the ones that were there would notice whatever I did. When the door rang next, I ran. "I'll get it." Nobody wanted to tell me not to, and nobody did, so I went and got it. Perhaps whoever was at the door would think I held some kind of special position in the gathering now. I was the welcomer, the first face, the new one, the one that we all came here to meet. I was so happy to see him. "Thank god you're here!"

Brad was the one who had invited me, and now he was there to tell them all so. He didn't, though. He just looked at me as if he didn't think I'd actually show up. "Can I take your coat?" I asked him.

"Uh, sure," he said. I hoped he was starting to question whether or not he was the only one there I knew, whether or not he had actually underestimated just how well liked I was, and that he had better start covering up the fact that he had only accidentally invited me, because the tides were turning in my favour and he'd better get on board. But then I stood there with the coat, not knowing where to go.

"Do you know where the bedroom is?" I asked.

"Uh, sure," he said again.

He would tell me where the bedroom was, and then I would take the coat there and take a minute to figure out what to do next. Maybe the bedroom was on the first floor and there would be a secondary door outside, maybe to a patio? And I would be able to escape without anyone seeing—except if there were a motion light. That would look awkward. If I just kept my face down, then maybe it would look like I didn't care if there were a motion light. I could just continue walking, as if I was going to my car or smoking a cigarette or something. Nobody knew if I smoked or not, or maybe they did. I didn't know.

Instead he started leading the way upstairs. That would be inconvenient, I thought, to have a patio door on the second floor of a house. Of course, there were balconies. I forgot about balconies for a second. A balcony is a second-floor patio, but only some of them have stairs that lead to the first floor, and there wasn't anything I could do, because he was going with me. When we got to the bedroom, there was nothing on the bed, because no one had started putting coats there. That was something, I guessed, that other people did, but apparently not here. They would know that I was an *outsider*.

When I turned around from setting down the coat, Brad was right behind me. "Did you come here just for me?" he asked.

"Yes," I said. I guessed that was a believable story. When they talked about it later, people would say that that girl had shown up, because Brad had invited her. She was Brad's new thing or something, or just some bitch he wanted to fuck, or maybe only half-wanted because there was nothing else around.

"Good," he said, and he kissed me. It was so wet in his mouth. I wondered how it was that he wandered about not drowning with all of that liquid in his mouth. It was unreasonable. A couple of times I had to wipe away my chin it was so wet. I thought I might drown if I didn't find a way to stop him.

I didn't know whether it was better to be thought of as his girlfriend or his whore. On the one hand, the girlfriend would be deceived, disappointed, constrained, and take it all in good stride because that's what good girlfriends do. The whore, on the other hand, was a whore. I thought that I preferred the latter, because I really didn't want to be deceived. Those were the options, though, deceived or mistreated or both. It really was a terrible decision, so I tried to go with both. I could be whatever I was supposed to be at the time. People had short memories, and there was no such thing as the collective consciousness. I could move from one group of people to the next, and the likelihood was that no one from the second group of people would ever know what I had done around the first group. It wasn't a spatial thing; it was the particular people that mattered. They were all stuck inside their own little heads and had literally no access to the heads of others where they kept their images of me, and I was eternally grateful for the finitude of humanity.

I knew the drill. When he reached up for my breasts I slipped myself into a more convenient position for him to do so, and when he reached for my pants, I helped him get them off. I didn't want him to be embarrassed if he couldn't figure out the zipper double button hook combination that kept them together. By now I was working automatically.

"You do this a lot?" he asked.

"What do you mean by a lot?"

"I don't know, a lot."

"I don't know what that means."

"It's OK, it'll be fine," he said. I wondered if he actually thought that I had failed to understand the concept of *a lot*, when what had just happened was that I had called him out on the fact that he had *no idea* how many people I should have or might have fucked before, and he didn't even know by what measure he would determine that. *That* was what *a lot* meant—*a lot* meant I should be blamed, and he could go fuck himself.

Where are all the women that the men are fucking? I had heard once that if you ask a woman how many men she had fucked, she would say three fewer than was true. And if you asked a man the same question (well, not the same, because it was *women* they were fucking), then they would say three more than was true. So what happened to the six people in between? Were men and women fucking the exact same number of people? Because that was the only way it seemed to work out. Otherwise, there was some poor woman somewhere getting fucked day in and day out by different men, actually a lot of women, if the numbers were to make sense. The women had to fuck less than the men, because society, but *that couldn't work*. Oh well. At least he felt better about himself for consoling me about the fact that I had never and would never consider what the actual definition of *a lot* was.

I didn't want to kiss him, so once he got my pants off, I lay on the bed face down.

"What are you doing?" he said. I thought quickly. I was either trying to get this over with, or I had no idea what I was doing. It was possible I had misread the whole situation, and that we weren't going to actually end up fucking. Was he rejecting me, at this late stage in the game? No, that couldn't be right.

"I want you to fuck me from behind," I said. I got up onto my knees and elbows and faced him, so he could see I was serious. A friend had told me once that if I ever found that a guy didn't want to fuck me immediately, I should just start masturbating. It was some kind of magic, I thought, even though I had never tried it. But it had been revealed as some kind of secret magic; I didn't have the guts to try it, though.

"Do you have a condom?"

"No, I don't care," I said. I'd been on the pill ever since *him*. I bought it from the nurse at the *secondary* school I attended. I looked at this Brad and figured that the kind of people he might have had the chance to fuck weren't the kind of people that carried anything. I didn't think, after that last question, that he would have the guts to visit a hooker or anything like that. He would probably think too hard about the fact that she was a human and then fail to get it up. That's the problem with humans, you can't just *fuck* them. (But they could.)

That was part of my power, I thought. I had suspected that women had more power than they let on, and it was confirmed once by my Biology teacher, who had once, after class, told me this little known fact that even though it seemed like the patriarchy ruled human society, especially in the West, it was actually always the woman who decided when to mate, whom to mate with, when and whose children to bear. It was the woman, and I thought it was a kind of power that I could use to make Brad forget the girlfriend I made up for him and just *fuck me* in this room of this weird house that I had just come to only half-invited.

"Come here," I said. Maybe that was easier for him.

And he did. He walked a little toward me, and I undid his pants. I pulled them down, because I didn't think he was small enough to angle through the hole without hurting him. I started feeling his cock up and down and looked him sincerely in the eyes. Then I licked it.

"Fuck me from behind," I said.

I turned around and faced away from him, waiting to feel him slide his dick into me. It seemed to take a little longer than usual, but it happened. I gently backed up and forward, doing all of the work for a few strokes until he caught on. I felt him awkwardly start grabbing at my hips, as if he wanted to but didn't know if he was allowed. I couldn't help because I was supporting myself on my arms, so I just let him flounder on that one.

"I want to see your face," he said.

"What?" I pretended not to hear and picked up pace.

"I want to see your face as I pleasure you," he said. It was one of the most disgusting things I had ever heard. I kept up the pace and hoped he wouldn't follow through. But Brad wanted to see my face, so he backed away from the edge of the bed and waited for me to turn over, like a gentleman. I turned over, positioning myself on the edge of the bed again.

"No, move back," he said. This was getting unreasonable. "I want to make love to you."

I wasn't sure where he'd heard that one or how he thought it possibly described what we were doing. Maybe if I started making noises he might finish more quickly, and I made a point of doing so. Brad was on top of me now, trying to stare deeply into my eyes as he slowly pushed his way in and then pulled out. Sometimes he pulled out all the way and couldn't find his way back in, so I had to grab his cock and ram it back inside. It was like being stabbed with a wet rubber hammer.

I closed my eyes and turned my head to the side as Brad's sweat dripped onto my face. Eventually, I felt a throbbing in my vagina, and Brad let himself lay down on top of me. "Well, I didn't think that was going to happen," he said. "I didn't think you liked me." When he pulled his dick out I could feel the goo oozing out of my vagina, and I felt bad for whoever owned this comforter. It looked like it was dry-clean only. I figured that Lizzie's family would blame Brad, because he was the one who invited me.

That wasn't true, though. They would always blame me. I was the evil temptress who practically let him fuck me.

"I don't actually like you," I said.

He seemed taken aback by that one.

"What? But you just…"

"That's not how it works. I just wanted to fuck you. That's why I came."

"I guess that's why both of us came," he said, trying to make an obviously lame joke, lame because of the fact that he thought I might have actually had an orgasm.

"Sure. Now when you go downstairs, could you send up your friend Chris?"

"What?" He sure said that an awful lot. Perhaps he was fucking stupid.

"Send up Chris. I want to fuck him too."

Again with the taken aback. I watched him put on his clothes, and I put on mine too, just in case this whole thing didn't work out. I had decided in definite favour of the whore. It was better to know better. I put my clothes back on and waited until he left the room before I looked around for a Kleenex box to wipe the junk off my vagina. Luckily, I found one. I didn't think Chris would come up, and I considered for a moment that he might see what state I was in, take one look at me and go back downstairs.

He was an asshole, and they all had to get fucked. Once, he had pulled out of me at the last moment and come all over my back. *God, you look like a slut,* he had said. *What the fuck part do you think you had in that?* I had wanted to say. But I couldn't say. I just had to take it and take it again and so that's what I would do.

Chris actually showed up. He didn't seem as awkward as Brad did. I guess Brad told him what the deal was, but I didn't think it would really sink in unless I did something about it, and so I lightly took him by the wrist, brought him all the way into the room, and kissed him once. Then I closed the door behind him and started to take off my clothes. I wondered if he wondered why I was wearing clothes at all, since I had just put them back on after fucking Brad, but it wasn't the first thing on his mind. The friend, the same friend who had told me to mastur-bate, had also told me once—men did not care about how many other men you have fucked. It was enough that you would fuck them. They made a big deal out of mine or yours or whatever they thought women were to them, but when it just came down to fucking, it didn't fucking matter.

I got down on my knees and grabbed Chris by the balls. I thought he would be surprised and delighted to see me on my knees; it made men feel powerful. It's like they didn't even know that I liter-ally had them by the balls. It was hard to maintain power when your soft parts are between someone's teeth, I thought. I wasn't going to bite down on them, but *I could*. At *any given time*, I could.

"Brad wouldn't fuck me from behind, so I want you do to it," I told him. It was the exact kind of stupid logic that he would believe. I thought I had gotten all of the paper bits off of my labia, but I turned off the lights just in case I hadn't. Well, the near light at least. The far light was far away, and there was no way to get there without ruining the moment.

Chris was more excited and managed to grab on tightly to my hips while he rammed himself in and out of me. I looked down at the pattern on the comforter and wondered if it would show stains. I thought I might get a similar one at home, except for the fact that I was sure Lizzie's parents would have paid a lot of money for it. I was always told that rich people paid more for things unnecessarily because they had to prove they were rich. That was wrong; they were buying better things. When I had a comforter that *looked* almost the same, I was always cold. It was polyester or something, and it had only two options: cold and sweat-cold. Sweat-cold happened when it was too warm and I sweat, and then the sweat made me cold. I doubted Lizzie was ever cold.

I wondered what the people downstairs thought, whether they were all talking about what I and Brad had just done, or whether he had told anyone at all except for Chris, or even if he told Chris. Perhaps he hadn't said anything but just sent Chris upstairs to the bedroom. It was more likely that he had told a few people by now, in order to explain what I was doing there at all. He had invited me, of course, so that I would fuck him.

I moved a little farther forward so that Chris would fall out of me, and then I turned around on the bed. I sat facing Chris where he stood and looked up at him from dick-height.

"Hit me," I said.

"What?" Jesus Christ it was like they were the same person.

"Hit me in the face, with your hand, like a slap. As hard as you like."

"What if someone sees?"

Were they all so stupid? There was no one on the second-floor patio.

He tried and failed, like he tried but he couldn't aim properly from such a great distance, and he just kind of winged me in the chin with his palm. I thought I might not want to give him pointers at this moment, so I avoided having to evaluate him by sticking his cock in my mouth again. It was harder now. I knew that I could deep throat it because *he* had always made me. Whenever my face got near his cock it stayed there. He held my face down there for what seemed like forever, but even though my face turned red and I started crying (and I knew I looked ugly crying), he always managed to come. I would have spit it out if there were anywhere polite to do it, but there never was. It was even worse after sitting in my mouth long enough to look around, so I got in the habit of just always swallowing.

Chris' semen was bitter and sticky. It kept coming even after I thought it was done, and some of it got onto my face and shirt. I thought I might really be attractive now. I was exactly the kind of woman men wanted me to be.

"So, how are you enjoying the party?" he asked. He was so polite.

"I don't really know anyone here," I said.

"Would you like to meet a friend of mine? I think he would like to meet you. I could send him up if you like," he said.

"Why the fuck not." I thought that came off a bit harshly. It wasn't his fault. I put my clothes back on again, found the Kleenex, spit on it and wiped off my face. I didn't want this new guy to feel anything sticky on my face. Once, I thought I had felt an orgasm. It was with *him*. We were smoking pot and I thought there might be something in it, because the sex felt *good*. After a while of his trying to get off on me I felt this wave go over my entire body and I didn't know if it was the drugs or the sex or what, but I thought it might be the only orgasm I'd had.

Chris kissed me goodbye and went back downstairs.

I sat on the floor leaning against the bed. I didn't know why, but I felt better the lower down I was in space. Of course, that wasn't true all of the time. When I was just wandering around like a regular person it didn't occur to me to *get low*. But when I was waiting for something or anxious about something else or dealing with any kind of indeterminacy, I liked to *get low*. Perhaps it was an evolutionary thing. When faced with the unexpected, get low. And then the predator wouldn't see you? That didn't make sense. You didn't get any smaller, just lower. You were just as visible. Ah, but the predator was used to looking for prey at eye level and so wouldn't think to look low. Did that make any sense? No. Predators would probably be hunting something smaller than they were, and so they would *start* by looking low. Perhaps I just felt badly about taking up so much vertical space. Perhaps I was too tall.

It was him. Jesus fuck I hadn't seen him for three years and it was him. There was some kind of mistake, perhaps; he had wandered in by accident. Someone else was coming, and then he would have to go. He would have to go when somebody else came. Or maybe I had made him up, I didn't know anymore. It was possible he wasn't actually there, that's all.

But he came into the room and said that Chris sent him. He said that he knew I was here and what I was doing and it didn't matter to him. He forgave me. *He forgave me. He forgave me.* I should be so thankful to him for forgiving me, because no one else would, I thought he might say next. He would be the only one capable of forgiving me, I was just that terrible of a person and he was so great that he could be the *only one ever* who might be willing to put up with me. He forgave me, and it was going to be OK because we were back together now. He understood why I would fuck other people because hey, I had needs (he thought I had needs?) and it didn't matter because *he forgave me*. He was kind of hoping not to have to do this at this party; he just wanted to have a good time with Chris and that was the plan. It wasn't all that kind of me to do this to him at this party, when he already had other plans, but *he forgave me for that too*.

I wasn't quite sure what to do with so much forgiveness. I was happy now that I was wearing clothes, because that would give me a few seconds, I thought. That would give me a few seconds to think of what to do and for fuck's sake *it was him* and *he forgave me*. He would not! I decided.

"You will not!" I told him.

"Will not what?"

"Forgive me."

"But I already have."

"You will not."

I thought if I could make it to the back of the door, I could grab the bathrobe. If I got the bathrobe, there would be a belt stuck in it, and I could use it to restrain him. *Fuck that*, I thought. Before he could figure out what I was up to, I was already at the bathrobe and pulling at the terrycloth belt. It stuck a little on the other terry cloth that makes bathrobes so comfortable, and it seemed like a very nice one at that. My own bathrobe was fleece, and it did nothing to absorb the water droplets still on my body when I exited the shower. If anything, it pressed it to my skin and made it worse. But Lizzie's father (must be her father) had a grey terry cloth bathrobe that was probably expensive (but not as expensive as the comforter), and I was going to ruin it.

I took the belt from the robe and looped it around his neck from the front. I had to do it from the front to get him in it. I moved around back. I put all of my weight into the back of his knee and he went down, but not far enough. He was six feet long but currently only about four and a half feet high, but that was still too much. On his knees he was taking up too much vertical space, and I couldn't let him. I aimed for the lower back and kicked him again. The only thing stopping him from going down entirely was the fact that I was holding his neck somewhat up with this terry cloth belt I had grown rather fond of. Perhaps if no one noticed I could take the whole thing home with me when I was done. Perhaps if no one noticed.

It took way longer than I might have expected, but I thought I got the job done. He looked worse than I did when I was crying, when his dick got stuck in my throat and he yelled at me for touching it with my teeth. It was his fucking fault, I thought, but I didn't say anything. It was his fault. For good measure, I kept holding him down with my foot and I started looping up the belt until it got even tighter around his neck, just like wringing the extra water out of something I had hand-washed. *It was him. It was his fault.*

It was he, I corrected myself. The nominative case? That seemed right but not, too formal for a murder, too good for him. He was him and nothing more and not even any more that. He could lay there and lie there. When they came to look, I would pretend he was so enthused by the sexual activity that he simply passed out, or perhaps he was into that fetish I had heard about with the strangulation. Perhaps it was an accident. He seemed like that type, now that you think about it. It didn't matter what I said, though, because the plan was to say it from very far away. Let them make some assumptions for a while, while I worked out the details.

The second-floor balcony did have a way down to the first. I thought that might work out well for Lizzie's family when they had backyard events, or perhaps it was a burden, since it meant that guests might think they were invited to the second floor when they weren't. In any case, I took those stairs down to the first floor and looked in the window. There they were, all fine; nobody was looking out. Perhaps they were too much in the light to see out into the dark. There was no motion light, as I had feared. It was just me and my grey terry cloth robe and the night.

SIX

I FIGURED that the crack in the wall wasn't anything particularly terrifying, since the house was at least forty years old, and since I realized that every house was basically a death trap anyway. A house always seemed to be something built, there already, something you were born into that stood up and outlasted everything in it. But once I went along with my father to a house that was being built, and I noticed how slipshod everything really was. Nails here and there, people who didn't really care, absolutely no attempt to account for the fact that the earth was in no way static. They would dig a hole in the ground and fill it with concrete, as if the bit of concrete was supposed to stop the ground from moving. But the ground did move; it always moved. It was just another case of man ramming something where it didn't belong. On the other hand, what else was I going to live in? It seemed to work perfectly fine for everyone. Except for some rare cases where building codes weren't followed and things fell down onto screaming children, it seemed to work perfectly fine for everyone.

I got used to the crack in the wall and used to stare at it. I thought that it might have gotten bigger, but there was no way to tell with it happening so gradually. I thought it might be like a path was formed. You couldn't see the path being formed but over time, a path would come and then everyone would know where to walk. And they'd walk there because other people had walked there, and that's how paths survived; that's what they fed on.

I had never had sex before I met him. He had, and told me as much, and that it was my responsibility to make sure not to let him have sex with me too. So it was up to me. It was my fault if anything happened, because I shouldn't have let him. I didn't understand what the big deal was. People had sex all the time, and it wasn't a big deal. Part of why I had sex with him was to prove as much. When I did it, it really wasn't a big deal.

We went to the drug store and bought some condoms; the ones with the spermicide, just in case they broke. He brought me to his parents' house, into the guest room. He shut the door, lifted up my dress, and rammed it in. It hurt, but it didn't take long to be over. After not very long, he heard his sister coming up the stairs and jumped off of me. He pretended to show me something he picked up off the shelf nearby, a yearbook. His sister came and opened the door; she reminded him he wasn't supposed to close the door when he had guests over. That was day six? I couldn't remember. He left soon after. After the sex, though, we went down the street to the coffee shop. He had chili. I hated it.

It was just so pathetic, and it smelled terrible.

Life smelled terrible. I couldn't get the smell off of
him afterwards. Maybe that's what went wrong;
maybe that's all that went wrong. I let him have the
chili, and he forever smelled of it. Chili and spermicide, and just human sweat; human sweat was
disgusting. Sometimes he would go for a couple of
days without bathing or changing his clothes. There
wasn't enough time for me to notice before then, but
eventually I would. I couldn't help but notice. He
was supposed to have gone away after that, but he
wouldn't make it.

I wore a low cut t-shirt, because a low cut t-shirt
was just about the sexiest thing I would ever think of
wearing. It would look too out of place to get done
up like some older woman; I would look ridiculous. I
was trying to look sexy, not ridiculous. So the t-shirt
it was. I had some left that were already wearing,
since the brand was discontinued. The sales girl told
me that they had received a lot of customer
complaints because when you bent over, even
slightly, people could see down your shirt. I knew
that; that's why shirts were low cut. I was just starting
to accept the fact that nobody gave a damn what I
thought or felt as long as they could see down my
shirt. If someone could see down my shirt, my feelings were valid and my thoughts important.

I didn't get to see the crack in the wall the first
time. Men had a thing, I thought, about bringing
someone home to their very own space. They would
go near, see how you fit in *close* to their space, and
then let you in it. If you didn't fit in *close by*, then you
were out, or at least not in. I got to the guest room
first, and then to his bedroom. So I went to the guest
room, and then the coffee shop, and then the
bedroom, where I saw the crack. I tried to catch it

getting bigger, like I imagined my vagina would have after his fiddling around down there, but no such luck.

"You said you were a virgin?" he asked.

"Yep."

"I kind of don't believe that."

"What's the problem?"

"The way you act. You don't act like a virgin. Plus, there was no blood."

I kind of didn't believe that he was actually doubting me. He smelled funny, and he doubted me. I saw a rolled up sweater in the corner and realized he must have brought it over from the other room. It wasn't just any old sweater; it had to be ordered in. It had to be ordered in, and he just threw it in the corner. He didn't even ask me what to do with it, he just threw it there and there it was.

"Well, you should believe me."

"OK I will, I guess."

"OK, good." But I knew he didn't.

When his sister went out, he wanted to do it again. It hurt, I told him. But it wouldn't this time, he said. He lied. I didn't know why I had believed him anyway; how was he supposed to know if I hurt or not? "I have to go to the bathroom," I said.

"Now?" he asked, mid-stride.

"Yes, now. Right now."

"Fine." He got up and turned on the television. He seemed a little pissed. I didn't think he should be pissed at all.

I went to piss. I had been holding it since before the guest room and it hurt too. I thought it might go away. People were always telling me that it wasn't a big deal; nothing was a big deal; I was making a big deal about nothing. So if it hurt, I figured it wouldn't soon. I started to wash my hands when there was a bang on the door. It startled me; I thought it might widen the crack.

"What are you doing in there?"

"Washing my hands."

"Come back already."

I wasn't quite sure what was happening. Was I supposed to wash my hands or not? A lifetime of primary school hygiene training had told me I had to, for at least twenty seconds, and especially if I was engaging in unhygienic activities, but then there was this guy on the other side of the door telling me to stop it. There was an internal voice versus an external voice, and you couldn't compare how loud they were because they were of different sorts. I made the decision based on which was more likely to have immediate effect—that was the guy at the door.

"I'm not done yet," he said.

"I know," I said.

Neither was really a statement, but each contained an implicit challenge. He wanted the pain to continue, and I didn't. I wanted to make him feel bad for the pain he had already caused, that he refused to believe was real. I wanted to get away from him and go back home. His breath smelled like spices I had always mentally associated with flatulence.

"Do you want to see the backyard?"

I did. So we went. Out the back of his house, there was a river. It was the same river that circled back under the bridge that led up to my house. It was about a twenty-minute walk straight through the centre of town. His bridge was a lot smaller. On my bridge, the railings were made of the same concrete as the bridge. It looked like it was poured from one giant bridge mold and crane-lifted into town. His was smaller, and the railings were iron. Maybe there was a time when his bridge had no railings, when they just trusted people to walk alongside it without falling in. It was possible, I thought. But then they had to add these railings. That didn't make sense, though, looking at it. They looked like they were stuck in the concrete when it was still wet. There was probably an anchor on the bottom of each one of those vertical posts, to hold it in place. I couldn't see them, of course, but I would assume as much.

"I'm cold."

"We'll go back in then."

I didn't want to go back in, I wanted to go home, but my sweater was still balled up in the corner, and if I never came back, I didn't want it sticking around. I imagined him smelling it and was disgusted by the image.

"I have to go to the bathroom."

"Again?"

"Yes."

I really did. I drank a lot of coffee. Once I had a gym teacher who refused to recognize the possibility that I would have to go piss in the middle of class. She claimed it was scientifically impossible for me to have gone to the bathroom right before class and to have to go again in the middle. She refused to let me go, but I went anyway. They called me down to the principal's office for pissing.

It hurt again, and I wondered if maybe he had torn something important, and if urine was getting into my bloodstream every time I went to the bathroom. I resolved to drink less coffee for the next few days while it healed, to slow down the progression of the poison. If it stung, it must be bad for it, I thought. I had always been told that urine was sterile, but if you walked into someone's house who had an incontinent cat, it sure didn't smell sterile. It smelled like something you didn't want getting into a fresh wound.

"What are you doing in there?" He called from the other side of the door.

"Can you come in here a minute?"

I was going to ask him about the stinging. He would know about these things, just like he knew that it wasn't really painful and that I shouldn't have let him have sex with me. *She let him. It was her fault.* I didn't know what was my fault, exactly. It seemed to be something that he promised was coming. It was strange how people did that; they could just announce what they were going to do, and if you didn't stop them, it was their fault. *You're going to make me X*, they'd say. And then they would X. And then it was my fault. Everyone agreed.

He was there.

"Have you ever used this straight razor?" I asked.

"No, it's my stepfather's."

"Oh, what razor do you use?"

He picked up a disposable from the counter. It was rusted through.

"Have you ever thought about killing yourself?"

"All the time," he said.

"Good," I said. "Good. Get into the shower with me."

I guessed he thought it might be fun? It might be. I turned on the water and without taking off my clothes, I got in. "Come on," I said.

Once, I had seen a movie, and I couldn't remember which one it was, but someone was shaving a woman's leg and seemed to think that was pretty sexy. It confused me; everything about sex that wasn't sex confused me. How did you figure out that you wanted to shave a woman's leg? I could figure out the penis-vagina thing. They liked being petted, so you might as well rub them together. But then there were all these things that were supposed to be sexy that had nothing to do with sex. It didn't matter. He took off his clothes and got in the shower.

Maybe he thought I was into some kind of sadism. I wasn't, probably. There was nothing sexy about it; people were even grosser on the inside than they were on the outside. Once you pierced the flesh bag, all of the gross things would start coming out. I imagined stabbing him in the stomach and watching a fountain of chili pour down his legs.

"I don't want to get old," I said.

"I'll still love you," he said. I kind of laughed.

"You won't. You'll grow tired of me and find someone else to fuck, and then I'll be old, alone, and fucked."

"I promise I would never do that to you."

"You have no fucking idea. You have no fucking idea what you will or won't do, because I get to decide. I get to decide what you will and won't do. It's not like these things are discrete events anyway. It's not like you say you'll love someone forever and then you do. It takes a long time—forever, in fact. And forever contains too many moments, too many to ever account for, and you're standing here promising me that for every single one of them, you'll love me. What does that even mean? What do you plan to do for all those minutes? What does *loving* me even mean? There's no action corresponding to that word, and you know as much. That's why you feel so comfortable making that promise to me.

There's nothing I can do to prove that at any given moment, you didn't *love* me. That's not really true, though, is it? There are a lot of things you would do if you *loved* me, but none of them is loving me itself. That's nothing; it means nothing. You mean nothing to me."

He looked at me, like he understood. He actually understood. He felt the way I did, and this was *his* way of pretending that it wasn't true. There was no such thing as forever; everything changed, everything wilted. He was disintegrating at a slower rate than his lunch was but disintegrating, nonetheless. When I disintegrated, there was a word for it: ugly. I didn't know how to be ugly, and I didn't want to find out. It meant that my feelings wouldn't be valid, and my thoughts would be unimportant. I thought maybe, if I went out right now, it wouldn't be so bad.

All of my life, I thought that death wouldn't be such a terrible thing. I wasn't old enough to be too attached to the physical world, and what I had seen of it, I didn't like. It was rough and stringy and full of plot holes. Everyone said one thing and did another, and I was supposed to pretend it was fine, or else *I* was the one who was not fine. Marilyn said in *The Misfits* that maybe you shouldn't expect people to keep their promises. Maybe it wasn't fair to them.

Maybe they shouldn't make promises. Maybe they shouldn't pretend that everything was *going* to be fine, as if *fine* was just around the corner in the next room, and if you could get there, it would just stay that way forever. Everyone's dream was eternity, and everyone's reality was just a moment on top of another one on top of another one, all piling up on one another until I had too many moments, I thought, too many, one on top of the other, crushing me. I knew it was too much to ask for them to stop, but that's all I could think about. Every moment was another moment and after that, another, and some of those moments were moments spent asking them please, to stop, but they wouldn't.

I didn't want to be there for the disintegration. I didn't want to know what it would be like to be disappointed, again and again, by the nature of everything that existed. That was the problem; by definition everything that exists exists, and that meant it was in some kind of persistent state while the moments dragged on by, tearing it apart. I was the thing that persisted. Everything got torn apart.

Some things started out that way. Most of what existed was never meant to be anything more than it was. I had seen that already. It was just there, taking up space, filling the time, and it didn't seem to care about the fact that it was falling apart. The crack didn't care if it took down the whole house with it. The house didn't care if it fell. The fact that the house seemed broken down meant that the house was still there to see itself fall apart. I didn't want to see myself fall apart. I didn't want, in the future, to think of this day and wonder what went wrong. How did it go so wrong? Why had I let it? *Everyone was disappointed by their first time*, I thought. If that were true, then why bother.

There was no need to go on, to exist. It didn't make anything better; it didn't get better. People got more used to it. They got used to the fact that they were disintegrating and they made light of it. The sweater in the corner would smell like me until someone either threw it out or took it in, and it would disintegrate either in the landfill or on someone else's body that was also disintegrating.

That's what sweaters *do*, they'd say. It was unreasonable of me to expect that anything should last forever, except for the fact that people kept promising it would.

They didn't know any better than I did, though. I couldn't believe their promises, because they didn't come from an informed standpoint. On these matters, my thoughts were just as valid as anyone else's. They had no secret information in their pocket assuring them of the fact that everything *would be* all right. There was no future if I didn't let it happen. What I felt most betrayed by, what I blamed him for, was pretending otherwise. He thought it would make everything better, but it just made everything worse. I would rather be right.

The alternative was to pretend along with him that anything is forever, all the while knowing that it wouldn't be. It would be a secret deal we made between us, each to assure the other that everything would be all right, each to pretend that we had the secret information that, if only the other knew, they would certainly be convinced. But of course I couldn't tell him what I knew. That was against protocol.

Fuck this, I thought, and slashed at his throat with the straight razor. It was the best way to disable him, I thought. I could still make it seem as if he had done it to himself. I wasn't sure if they could tell in which order the wounds were made, but I knew that they wouldn't try that hard anyway. As he grabbed his throat, I slashed at his wrist too. That would be enough, I thought, to allow some good man to put in a hard day's work concluding that a troubled boy committed suicide in the strange house on Earl Street. That would be enough. I turned on the shower just in case; maybe they could see how much farther the neck blood flew compared to the wrist blood. I wanted him in a bathtub full of water when they got there.

There were sounds, but I knew they would be over soon. That's the only thing that made them bearable. I imagined having to hear those sounds forever, and what kind of torture that would be. The thing about them was that they wouldn't, though, they wouldn't last forever. So on I went. I put the old rubber plug in the drain and hoped that it would hold until they got there, to see him in the puddle. He belonged in a puddle. He belonged in a puddle forever. I thought of how you could be one thing and then suddenly, as if from nowhere, become another and then forever. *But there was no such thing.* I could never be a virgin again, and that was fine. He couldn't be alive again, and that was fine. Everything was fine, because even the disintegrations didn't last forever. He was basically a puddle already, if you thought about it.

I thought the water would have rinsed my clothes enough, but they left a red wet trail as I tried to maneuver around the house. I went back to his room and got the sweater. If I stood in the river a while, I thought, it might rinse out my clothes enough for me to go home. I thought about the river water and how much it might sting. I would leave the sweater near the edge so I would have something dry to put on afterwards. Maybe I could take off the t-shirt I was wearing and just let it float away. That might make a nice picture, I thought. If only I had a camera, I could take a picture of it floating away; then it would remain, as an image, as a still shot of a moving thing. *But images die too.*

SEVEN

SOMETHING WAS DIFFERENT THAT DAY. I could feel it. The rain prevented the day from ever getting light, and it was as if the night were continuing. I had to be somewhere, but it was the middle of the night. Everyone else would be going out too, though, I thought. That would make it seem less odd.

On my way out the door the key stuck again, and I made a note to go back to the machine to have another one printed. Of course, if the second one were made on the model of this one, it might be just as bad or worse. I had the original, though. If I made a copy of the original, then it should turn out exactly like this one, so just as bad. I made a note to go find the original so I could make a key just as bad as the one I had but maybe not worse.

There was salt all over the sidewalk; it was going to stain my shoes again. I hated having to talk to people who would know I had been walking outside. I didn't like anybody knowing anything about anything. Still, it's not as bad since I bought the car. I used to have to walk along the edges of the roads where there were no sidewalks. By the time I got to work I would have mud on my shoes, which would form a trail directly to my office if I didn't have time to go to the restroom and clean them on the way in. If I did, it could have been anyone going from the outside to the restroom. Of course, some perceptive individual might have seen the trail of mud flakes leading to my office at some point or another and made a mental note that I was always the one with the muddy shoes. If that were true, then I would be blamed for all of it, all the time. What about the times it wasn't me, though? That didn't seem fair.

Some salt didn't seem so bad, in light of things. The car was old but went. I shouldn't have bought it; it was too old. I didn't seem to think it mattered. Like people, cars would age at different rates, I thought. There were some people, you could tell, who were going to die early. You could see it in their faces. There were other people who were going to live a long time; they looked younger. That's what they would say. But they were only younger on a model of linear time; according to the time relative to their own degradation, they were just as old as they should be. The car was just as old as it should be, except that in linear time it was over ten years old.

I was to give a talk today, well, one of the talks today. I would be part of a panel on something I had no idea how to talk about, but I trusted my own ability to appear as if I did. That was the key to things; appear as one did. It was some week celebrating thing, and I would talk to them about it. I would take cues from the faces of the people in the room and then tell them things they liked. Everyone would feel nicely about it; that was the key to things. There was no great logic to it, no standard evaluation of what made something good or not good, no judge to say whether or not I had done well or not done well. I used to try to replace that absentee judge with *him* (or indeed, him, or him, or him), but now I reminded myself that none of them, not a one, had any authority on the topic (any topic). I might as well be the one who decides. It was exhilarating at first, then it became a habit of hopelessness. There was nothing to aim for; no matter what I chose, it would never be *it*.

I wondered if that's why people ended up having children. It was probably the case that, finding nothing, they aimed for some purpose outside of themselves that would stop the constant gnawing of dejection. Knowing that there was nothing but other people, other people just like me, him, them, other people could be the only purpose. So make one, why not. I didn't think this thought process was explicit by any means. Certainly no one I had talked to about it would admit that children were a backup plan to achieving universality.

That's what I was thinking when I walked into the room at the University library. Maybe it was that thought, or maybe it was the lighting, but I swore I saw him.

It couldn't be, I thought. It wasn't. There he was— a skinny but broad-shouldered teenager with dark blond, close-cropped curly hair, dimples and bags around his eyes from not sleeping. There he was, just sitting there, pretending as though he belonged. He couldn't. He couldn't have just shown up without knowing I would be there. He acted as if he did, though.

He acted suspiciously as if he were up to nothing. Sitting there, in the room lit by fluorescents, I tried to squint in order to make it seem as if he weren't well-lit, perfectly lit, just sitting there, acting as if he weren't. He didn't notice when I came in; he also didn't do anything else. He didn't sit there, playing with his phone. He didn't sit there, reading a book to pass the time. He didn't look around the room as if he were bored and waiting for an excuse to exit. He didn't angle himself towards the door as if he were waiting for someone to join him. He just sat there. It was painful to look at; there was nothing his eyes seemed pointed towards. Usually, if you looked at the direction of the eyes, you could see where they were pointing and therefore the intent of the individual inside. But he wasn't looking in any direction; it was the most amazing thing. It was like he wasn't in there; he wasn't inside; he wasn't there. But there he was.

It was definitely *him*. How could it be, though? When I had seen him last, almost twenty years ago, he was young. He was still young. Perhaps I was getting old and thought everyone else was young. I looked around the room to confirm; no, everyone else was just as old as they should be. I looked back at him and tried to discern some small difference, some difference between him and my memory of him in order to distinguish the two properly into distinct individuals. I had thought about how something maintains identity over time, but it was always in relation to the fact that, no matter what you did, things seemed to change. Some things grew while others disintegrated. A plant is the same plant as the seed, even if they look different. A man is the same as a man once was even if he were older—because he is older. If he were not the older version of the young man then there would be nothing to which he would be older. Precisely because we say he is "older", he is the same man as the younger. But *he* was not older, not even a little.

That's why, I thought, my thought-tangent might have something to do with it. I wasn't being deceived or anything like that, but my thoughts had found their way out into the world and had assured the fact that when I arrived, not *he*, but *his child* would be there. I had never had it, though. I wondered who did, and what he was doing there. Was it an accident? If only I could find some difference between them, then I could explain why this one here was a younger version of that one, not in the sense of being identical over time, but in the sense of being a copy of the first, a genetically mixed copy, for somewhere, there had to be a mother. Where was her hair, her eyes? What had he done to her eyes that they wouldn't have been passed on? What had he done to her, and where was she now?

It didn't make any sense for me to be there now. It was probably just a freshman, he was probably just a freshman. That put him only slightly beyond the time I still heard about him, or possibly just before. If it were before, that wouldn't make any sense. If he were slightly beyond, I thought it might be possible. But the searches turned up nothing. There was no marriage, no death, no announcement of a child, nothing. If he were *his* child, certainly *he* would have had to have done something noteworthy, something I would have found out.

Maybe I had had his child. It was one of the only theories that seemed to make sense. I had borne his child way back when, and had somehow forgotten about the whole incident. I did it, and then he made me disappear. He stole my memory, my thoughts, everything I had to do with the incident, and even the genetic material from the child we had made together. That's why he didn't have my eyes, or my hair, or anything of mine. He had taken it all back, somehow. He had it somewhere, and was doing who knew what to it. He had used it to make this copy of himself that ensured he would remain, in a sense, young (or at least younger), and this copy knew nothing of it but had just gone to the library like any normal young person might.

It didn't seem plausible, except for the fact that there was nothing he seemed to be looking towards. I wouldn't be looking towards anything either if I had any inkling that I were just a copy-spawn of a terrible man who didn't know any better about what he had done.

Maybe it was more general than that; maybe I had just met one instance of the terrible man when in fact there were many, distributed throughout time and space, under the assumption that no one would notice if someone appeared to be someone else somewhat older than they themselves were. They weren't clones, or anything silly like that. They were the physical manifestation of evil, ignorant of their own state, killing everything they could and believing they were just as anyone else. They couldn't see outside of their faces with those dead eyes, and so they didn't know just how far they had differed. Once this young fellow had met a man, I imagined, who appeared much like him but older. They marveled at the resemblance and made the only reasonable conclusion—that it was coincidence and happenstance. They didn't have anything to talk about, really, because they lived separate lives. After a few short moments, they went their separate ways.

He might not have even told anyone about it. Perhaps he had no one to talk to.

Maybe he was already dead; maybe that spot was reserved for *his* preserved corpse, which sat there, sitting in on lectures all day, learning nothing. That would explain the eyes but not the motion; occasionally, he would shift a little in the seat or make some other non-intentional action that didn't seem to accomplish much. Maybe he was brain dead; he was brain dead and they let him sit in the seat because they thought it would make him feel good to seem like a normal boy. He didn't have the wherewithal to look in a direction, but he would still feel good about that, advocates would say.

Others would say it was a cruel torture to the poor brain dead boy who didn't want his lack of potential thrown in his face every day. Maybe it was *him*, and he was brain dead. The brain death prevented his aging, and it happened to be the case that it happened just after, shortly after, I had seen him last. That would mean so many things—that the brain was responsible for time, for one. Not just the perception of time, we already know that, but for time itself. That which did not brain would not time. But that didn't make any sense either. Plants at least did something, and you could see what they were up to. They made intentional movements; they aimed at the sun, they grew towards water. The plants did so much more than he did, and they didn't have brains at all. It just couldn't be right.

It was weird how he would move; it wasn't like he reached for something or tried to make himself more comfortable. He just *moved*. I hadn't seen anything like it before. He looked but not *at* and he moved but not *towards* or even away. Even if this were some happenstance boy in a coincidental room, there was something devastatingly wrong with him. I looked around to see if others had noticed it too. They just went on. At least they went on in a comprehensible manner. Perhaps *that* was it. He could not move or look in a comprehensible manner, because motion *towards* meant the advancement of time. That would be it, I thought. Of course, it seemed pretty self-defeating. Why bother eliminating time if there were nothing to do outside of it.

He wasn't doing *anything*. What happened when he did do something? Would time start again? That might be what he was doing. He was saving his moments, throughout his life, avoiding time by moving nowhere and towards nothing. He was saving them for now, when he would reveal himself to me and *ta-da*, we would have the longest possible time together, now that he had restarted time again. You would think that he might have let me in on the secret before, so that we might be of similar ages when it was time. Of course, that would ruin the surprise. Of course, if he suggested it, I would have said no. He was a terrible fucking person.

It didn't matter now, it was time to start. Luckily, I had gotten so used to rambling on in classes in order to fill the time periods that today I didn't have to think in order to speak. I thought about the different stages of the transmission of thoughts into speech. Some thoughts were thought and not spoken. Some thoughts were thought about and then spoken. Other thoughts did not seem to be thought *until* they were spoken. Sometimes, words were used when there were no thoughts. Maybe that's what people meant when they said that they didn't mean what they said—that there were literally no thoughts that they intended to be put into words. I thought it more likely that they did mean what they said, in the sense that they were sincere. They just weren't honest. Honesty required an objective state of affairs to correspond to one's thoughts or speech in order to make them true, and people were deluded. They couldn't be honest, because they were people.

The only thing that people have in common is that they die. I wondered if he *could* die. If he couldn't, that would mean he was not a person. If he wasn't a person, what was he doing in the University's library at all? Even the most mystical of my explanations depended on the idea that he was a person. If he wasn't, then perhaps it wasn't *him*. *His* humanity was always evident, always thrown in my face or wherever he felt like throwing it. It was the worst part of humanity that poked me in the leg or the back or that he thrust into my hand. The worst part of humanity was constantly demanding attention.

If he could die, then all would be right again. I would be happy with the conclusion that something, one thing, was accurate. I could come up with several explanations for what had happened, all premised on the certain conclusion that he was human, and then when asked to explain, I could confidently state that the true explanation was one of *X, Y, or Z*. And if any one of X, Y, or Z were true, then that statement would be true. If it weren't, I could continue to add letters on until it were true, a near-infinite number of letters. If he were human and there were a finite number of explanations for his being that rested on his humanity, then it would all logically work out.

I thought, for a second, that maybe I shouldn't.

Maybe it was the case that his current state, with the eyes and the movement, was the result of a long and arduous process meant to eliminate his demands on me and the world. If he didn't act out towards the world, then that would eliminate his possibility to harm it. That didn't explain the time thing, though. If there was anything certain, it was this thing's monstrosity, not its humanity. So I had to kill it, because it was monstrous, in order to prove that it was human. It all worked out if you thought about it.

I lingered in the room, staring at it. It hadn't done anything the whole time; it didn't speak, it didn't look, and it didn't do anything. It was possible that it had died during the proceedings. If it were dead already, I wouldn't have to kill it. That much was certain. I tried to find some evidence of the idea that it was experiencing time. If it were quiet enough, I thought, I could hear a heartbeat. If it weren't for the consistent hum of the universe coursing through the walls of the place, I might be able to hear its existence in time. But I couldn't.

Of course it was breathing. It had to be breathing. If I got close enough, I could smell the stale breath of the monster who hadn't drunk anything in a while and whose mouth water was starting to rot. I would be able to smell it on his breath, then, if he were existing. I didn't want to get very close to it, though. It seemed to have this thing about it that demanded a minimum spatial distance. Nobody had even sat near it the whole time, it was so obvious. At the same time, no one took note of it.

Maybe it wasn't there. Maybe I was the only one who had seen it, and it was time to go home, make dinner and feed the cats. That was my last working theory. If I could get by it, then it couldn't stop me and remain consistent with what it had done so far. It would be out of character for it to stop me. Of course, that didn't mean anything. At the same time, I wanted to know for certain that it didn't exist. There didn't seem to be any way to avoid it and also confront it.

I took the microphone with me, just in case. It was the heaviest thing I could find that wasn't nailed down to anything else. I didn't think of bringing my regular bag with me. I was just going to wing it, after all. Bringing a bag would make it look like I was dependent on additional material things for my existence. Extra things were perceived in my circles as a vulnerability, I thought. If I could just exist on my own merit, I wouldn't need a whole extra set of things to carry around. I would just go. So I did. And I grabbed the microphone, because it was not attached to anything, except for the sound system where the cord was plugged in. If I stretched it too far, it would come unplugged. I was thankful that the room wasn't mic'ed up like my regular one. This thing wasn't going to be pinned to anyone's lapel. It was the sort they used years ago. I thought of an old announcer sitting at a table, narrating some sporting event, maybe a horse race, stuck to the table because that's where the microphone was. The library must not have dedicated any of their budget to improving their sound system. Libraries were supposed to be quiet, after all.

Trying to look like I was meant to have that microphone, I got up and maneuvered to its general vicinity. So far, so good. It didn't look at anything or move in any direction. It kind of vibrated a bit. I wasn't sure if that was evidence of its existence or non-existence, so I kept going. For as long as I was in front of it, I watched it. I thought as soon as I was past, I could stop looking at it, and then it would be gone. I didn't account for any delay, though, in how long it should take to move past it, or how far I had to be from it in order for it to go away. There must have been some kind of lag, though, because when I moved past it, it reached out. It seemed to grab me without meaning to; it latched on without wanting to, and it spoke but not to me.

Bah buh bah buh buh buh... Pah!

That certainly didn't mean anything. I hit it. I hit it in the face, aiming for the mouth to make it stop. If I could disable the face, the arm would stop gripping me, and I could go to where it didn't exist. If the face would just *look* somewhere, *look*. It hurt me without even looking, without even meaning to. It just latched on with its nonsense syllables and now I *had* to kill it, to make sure it was dead. It wouldn't give up, though. It wouldn't let me go. I hit it and hit it and heard the microphone echoing through the speakers, *thump thump thump* like a heartbeat echoing across the walls and filling the room. The room was alive but he wasn't and wouldn't be soon.

EIGHT

THE WORST THING about children was that just about anyone could have them. There was something to be said for the things that *not* everybody could do, I thought. I thought about how inauthentically people recognized at once the fact that their children were not the only children in the world, nor even close to the objectively best children, and yet they loved those children as if they were the best things in the world. That was a strange equation for value. There was a strange equation for value in general, when it came to children.

Have children, an older woman had once told me when I was working in an office, entering data. *Have children*, she said, as if she were imparting some kind of secret knowledge that I myself did not know. You were supposed to rely on that kind of secret knowledge to trust those people and do what they said, even though those people and what they said made literally no sense. Maybe it had something to do with the fact that there was a time limit on it. If it was a limited time offer, I would have to call now to get in on the deal. Call now! Get knocked up. There's no going back.

To say that having children was something that just about anyone could do, I thought, wasn't really fair. What about the people who couldn't have children? Should they be so harshly blamed for not even being able to do a simple thing that most other people do just by accident? Surely not. It also wasn't the case that you should then value the ability to have children, for the sake of the people who couldn't. It still wasn't anything special. There was no value to be attributed either to the people who could have children or the people who couldn't.

Of course, there were the indefinites. I was an indefinite. I'd never gotten pregnant, so I thought there might yet be some hope that I couldn't. If I couldn't get pregnant, then no one could blame me for not wanting to get pregnant. It would eliminate the option. Of course, I could always adopt. That would negate the whole time limit problem, and therefore the overvaluing of children in general. I wondered why more people didn't do that, instead of being sucked in to the limited time offer and condemning themselves to the life of a nurse-maid.

There was the argument that having children ensured your own immortality. If that were so, then it was definitely a sort of personal immortality. They would literally preserve your genetic material in a new host, carry on your vices, and fuck up the next generation just like you fucked them up, until they came to a realization in their thirties that it was all your fault and made a pointless effort to change. I wasn't interested in personal immortality. Personal immortality just resulted in more people; I wanted to be better than that.

No one remembered you for having children. It wasn't like you went to school and learned the great canon of people who went on to have good children. No one gave a fuck what Dostoevsky's mother's name was; no one was congratulating her on having such great children. Well, maybe when she was alive they did, but more likely not. He did go to prison, after all. I would rather go to prison than have children, and that was that. The whole thing was just so human. Stick thing A into thing B, rub until the goo shoots out, try to catch it as best you can, provide it with a loving home and invest early so that it can go to a good school and learn about all of the people who didn't condemn themselves to the life of parenthood, i.e., the death of immortality.

There were very few times when I was concerned about controlling the body. I knew that, in a pinch, I could very well control just about everything my body tried to do to frustrate me. When I was sick, I could drag myself out of bed and to wherever I had to go, and even act normally enough to get by. When I was drunk, I could still put my words together and force one leg after the other to get where I was going. When I got a migraine that time during a reading group, I pretended that I could still read the words on the page, even though they were covered in a shimmering grid. I had never lost control of the body in any meaningful way, and since most of my body parts were under the direct control of my will, I didn't worry about it most of the time. Most of the time, body parts could be separated into two possible categories: those that could have an effect on the world around them (eyes, arms, muscles in general, perceptual organs in general), and those that didn't. Those that didn't were generally unfelt; it was as if they weren't there. Only when they were disturbed could you start to feel them and what they were really up to. There was the one responsible for the bile I threw up, and there was the one that stayed fuzzy long into the afternoon if I took too many pills the night before. They resisted, but they would fucking submit if I put them up to it.

Of course, I couldn't control my body's reactions to external things—sometimes. I had fallen on the ice quite a few times, which some might blame me for, but in general my recovery skills were good enough. There was nothing like giving a knockdown knockout knocked up argument for something to a roomful of people and then falling over. The former capacity indicated a worldliness on the part of the subject, while the latter indicated that still, they hadn't learned to use their legs. I had learned to use my legs just fine, thank you. Besides, I didn't have to use them that often or for much.

He would put his knees down on my thighs so that I couldn't move them. I tried to figure out the physics of it once, just how much force I would have to exert and in what direction in order to unsteady him, but it was years too late by then. Men had a higher centre of gravity, while women shut the fuck up and waited for them to get it over with. Then I was like a kid with jam hands; I couldn't move or touch anything without getting everything everywhere, and of course I was the one to blame for that too, just like they were.

Every time, I could feel them swimming, unless he used a condom. When he got sweaty enough, I could start to feel them swimming, and I would picture the images from the videos they presented in Sex Ed class about what happened when you had sex without a condom. I wondered if sex with a condom really counted; after all, you weren't really touching the person. At the same time, you couldn't distinguish sex without a condom from sex with a condom if sex with a condom didn't count. There would just be sex, no condom implied. I thought of all of the terrible names people came up with for having sex, like making love or porking, riding bareback, bumping uglies. How could anyone have sex after hearing it described with words like that? Nobody wanted to do that. But I had to, and when I did, I could always feel them swimming.

Usually, they died after a while. I could stop feeling them swim around in there; it was like the feeling you'd get looking at a bowl full of writhing tadpoles, I thought, not that I'd ever seen anything like it. It was easy enough to picture, though. I didn't know if tadpoles could live that close together in a bowl, but it definitely wasn't like writhing snakes. Writhing snakes would be too dry; they would maintain separation, whereas the tadpoles would form into one giant wet heat where there was less of a distinction between where one ended and the other began. That's what gave rise to the general unrest and feeling of unwellness that resulted from the tadpoles. They would swim too far apart and take in extra air, or they would swim too close together, and the whole pile of them seemed to get dense. When I read the ancient medical texts, I thought they might be on to something. I thought it might have been Hippocrates who recommended to a prostitute that when she thought she might have been impregnated, she should jump up and down until the semen came out. If the semen came out, everything was fine, but if it got stuck up in there, you might get pregnant. I couldn't remember, though, who it was.

I thought it much more important that the universe know of my intention not to take on this additional pile of human goo that threatened to ruin me. If I jumped up and down, I thought, the universe would see and would bend to my will. That, in addition to the birth control, worked so well that I still didn't know if I was even capable of getting pregnant. Perhaps not. Still, I counted getting pregnant as one of the things outside of my control, and I therefore had to be very careful.

I had felt, for over a year since he'd finally let me go, that mangled knot of tadpoles. It refused to come out, and it refused to die. It didn't get any bigger; it just kind of stayed there, waiting for its chance. I didn't know what it was waiting for, or what it would do when that happened, but I figured its plan was probably to latch on for dear life and wait it out. It was in hibernation, or some form of stasis, just hiding out inside me where I couldn't reach it or make it fall out or kill it. It was just there, wriggling. I thought once, in desperation, that maybe if I let another man fuck me, his semen might take offense to that already present. There would be a fight to the death, and each would kill the other off. That didn't seem to work, though. It didn't get bigger, or smaller, or die, or anything. Nothing I did seemed to have any effect. I got used to it. If I tried, I could still feel it there, but when I wasn't trying, it would fade into the background. It was like forgetting about your toes outside in the winter and then wiggling them, just to see if you could still feel them. At first they would move, but the feeling wasn't there in full effect. After trying a bit, I could feel it just as well as I ever could. I could smell it too.

The people at the drugstore are particularly annoying for the fact that whenever you go to buy something from them, they pretend not to be judging you. You'd think they would get used to it, day after day, another this, that, pregnancy test, but they didn't seem to. Perhaps that was because they kept getting new employees. People kept breeding, and there was always some part-time fuck at the cash whose uncle had an uncle who was an assistant to the manager, and they hadn't worked there long enough not to pretend not to be judging you. They probably put it right in the training—when someone comes up with something objectively embarrassing, like a pregnancy test, you should make a show of pretending as if you don't care what it is. That will make them feel better, those god damned knocked up sluts. You should be sensitive to the purchasing habits of knocked up sluts; corporate thought it was a good business tactic.

I had bought pregnancy tests several times. Even when I felt no distinctive difference, I often worried. I thought I had a right to worry. Imagine something that other people are doing literally all of the time, and then consider indeed just how disanalogous you were to those people—not enough—and then consider how likely it was that you were doomed to abject servitude in the face of someone whose best hope in life would be to outperform you, to have you forgotten, lost in the annals of whatever human records continued to exist. When you considered how many forgettable people there were, it wasn't a surprise that most of them were immediately forgotten. *Jane, was born, had a kid, kid's still alive, kid let a stripper touch his dick last week while his wife thought he was buying milk, he'll die soon too*, said all of the obituaries.

The first time I bought the pregnancy test, I did a quick calculation. There were two possible outcomes of the test, so there was only a fifty-percent chance I was pregnant. That seemed like too high of a chance, but when I considered that I would only be taking the test if I had a suspicion that my body had been invaded by foreign DNA, then that seemed to lean towards the fifty-percent positive side. And taking into account the fact that I was ovulating probably ten percent of the time, and that it only took one tadpole out of the fucking waves of them that he kept shooting at me, it seemed almost certain that I was doomed. But it came out negative. Over the next few years, I tested intermittently, whenever I felt like I needed the certainty of it more than I abhorred the inconvenience of going out, buying the test from some douche who couldn't even count change properly, having to ask for a bag like the request was something so fucking out of hand that I should be ashamed of myself for that alone, taking it somewhere, pissing on the stick, waiting for the piss stick to mature, and then hiding it in some garbage that I didn't think anyone would go through. That was the problem with people, I thought, they were all potentially the kind of people who would go through your garbage and find your piss stick. They lived in garbage; they were made of it. I could feel it.

After all of this time, I was relatively certain that it would come out negative. After all, all of the previous tests had come out negative, which made the likelihood that this one would change that streak one out of all of them. The likelihood wasn't that high. Plus, I hadn't had sex in over a year. It was going to be negative, I thought, but I couldn't be certain. I thought that sometimes the laws of physics have changed just to fuck with me, to make me look like a crazy person. The rules of biology couldn't be all that different; on most theories, biology would be reducible at some point to physics. It was just a living physics, really.

I knew who the father was. It was him, obviously. His semen had never gone away but was waiting there, waiting for an opportunity. It found a way to nourish itself using me as a host and it lived there, waiting to meet the right ovum. It all sounded so disgusting; I wondered how I had let it go on as long as I did, and then I remembered that I could forget about it, if I wanted to. Of course, if I wanted to, then I couldn't. Conception was like a miniature version of what happened between the people. After the people had gone through the initial screening process and decided to rub genitals, the sperm had to see if there was anyone inside whom they felt like squirming their way into. It was a whole other, secondary process, and way more skewed. Compared to the millions of sperm waiting around to penetrate whatever they could penetrate, the ova were so much more selective. Every month, a debutante would be released at her very own debutante ball and then she would be worked over by everyone in the room until she either got fucked to death and was ejected in a mass of blood or found a nice young man to take up residence with in someone else's body. Maybe humans were doing that on the earth; maybe the earth was right now conducting its own panicked pregnancy test to make sure she hadn't met anyone nice lately. Of course, from within my own puny human viewpoint I couldn't possibly imagine what that would look like, and I didn't think I should be blamed for that failure, either.

Maybe that's what his mother was trying to do. They had found her, stabbed, in her bedroom. Maybe she was trying to give herself a very late-term abortion —ten years too late, from the sounds of it. I wouldn't make that same mistake, I told myself. I would succeed where his mother had failed.

The test was positively positive. I tried to think to myself that it was a failed test, but I knew that false positives were not the one percent margin of error that the box claimed the test to have. There were false negatives, because the test failed to pick up on early pregnancy hormones; there wasn't enough of it to make the test turn positive. If the test was positive, though, it was positively positive. I knew the test wouldn't fuck with me. I thought about how uncertain I was about the laws of procreation and how certain I was in the reliability of a plastic stick and decided that my incongruencies were hilariously charming. Also, I had to kill it.

I didn't have to kill it because it was a bundle of cells; I had to kill it because it was *him.* It was going to be a human; it was set on that course, despite everything I had done. Despite all of the pills and the jumping and the celibacy it had still gotten in; it had wormed its way in and if I didn't kill it now, it would never leave me alone. I was sick of having him around. If I killed it properly, I thought, then maybe even that squirming feeling would go away. I would finally be free; and even if the test were inaccurate, if my test was the one in a million false positives corresponding to the one in a million sperm that was shacking up with my ovum, I could still get rid of that constant feeling of inner movement that had been fucking with me the better part of ten years.

While I had often blamed his mother, I now felt we finally had something in common. We were both pregnant with him. Where his mother had failed, she was too late, I would succeed. He would not gain personal immortality. It was interesting how they actually believed that you could achieve personal immortality through having children and also *die*. That didn't make any sense. If the opposite of life was death, what was the opposite of immortality? Mortality, obviously, but mortality meant both life and death. It didn't make any sense.

The test was a battle cry from within; after years of lying in wait, it decided now would be the time to strike. I wondered what I had done to make it think that now was the time. It could be like an opportunistic virus. When the immune system was down, it would know it was time to strike, live on, use me for its own means. This thing was the same, whatever it was. It couldn't have been fine; there was no way that anything people would consider normal would pop out of my vagina in several months' time, not with a conception like this one. I had to do it, I thought, to prevent that future evil, whatever it was. Of course, a future evil wasn't a real evil yet, so nobody would have to worry about it. What kind of person doesn't worry about the future? It was the only thing to worry about; it was the only thing that could be changed.

I had to do it, to avenge myself. Of course, with that motivation, one had to assume that the thing I was killing had wronged me personally. Of course, it had. It had lain in wait inside my person and then latched on, hanging on for life as I tried my best to evict it. I pictured it, hanging on to my cervix like someone falling over the edge of the cliff in a movie, hanging on by just the fingertips. Usually, those people survived. *Not this time.*

His mother probably had gained some secret knowledge, and that's why she went for the kitchen knife. I finally understood why she had done what she had done, how it was necessary. It was the only way to kill him. It was ten years too late for the both of them, and the only way to get rid of it now was to break it into small parts and then kill those off one by one. Divide and conquer. Divide, divide, divide.

Divide, divide, divide, I thought, and stabbed diligently into the area that the diagram had indicated my uterus would be. *Divide, divide, divide.* I didn't know how many pieces it would have to divide into before it would be incapable of recombining into something terrible. I hoped I would stay conscious long enough to feel it stop its wriggling. *Divide, divide, divide.* I thought I would survive the wounds. I wasn't stabbing anything important. His mother had done it.

I saw the blood coming out, but it didn't seem solid enough to be *him*. He was always rigid when he was inside of me, and it didn't make sense that he would be any different now. So I kept at it, waiting for the chunks of him to come back out. If I could just make it come out, I could carry on, just like the story of Hippocrates' happy prostitute.

NINE

IT WAS PROBABLY STILL TOO EARLY. I wanted to go to the store, but it was still a little too early. I would go after dark; after dark everything was different. There were different people out. Everyone I knew would be locked up inside. I would have to sleep through the morning, as usual, but I would still have the crossover in the afternoon to deal with the day world. From morning to afternoon, I slept, from afternoon to evening there was the world, and from evening to morning there was the darkness. What was special about the darkness was that during the day, everyone forgot about it.

When it got dark too soon, it didn't count. That is, in the winter, when it got dark earlier than it should, people pretended it wasn't dark yet and just carried about their business. They continued going to stores, having their dinner, even though it was as dark as it was ever going to get. I couldn't function in that mid-range of darkness. The interference was still there. You could hear people doing things, and they would take up all of the thinking space.

The idea was that thinking couldn't take up space, and that was technically accurate. The thoughts spread out like the intersections on a grid. The grid itself was nothing, it was made of things— roads and trees and what they called intersections, which was really just two roads, or one road that continued meeting with another that had a break in it. People would say it was where two roads met, but there weren't two roads stacked on top of one another or anything silly like that. The space in which thoughts existed wasn't the space in which things existed. It was a sort of meta-space that you could abstract from the space in which things really existed. And it could hold time.

Meta-space was where temporally distant things continued to exist. They were there in the sweater, in the car, in the house on Earl Street, in the tree out back. It was the space on top of space—the second road that had no physical part to it, even though everyone would admit that it was *there*. When you came to an intersection, you didn't drive off Main for a second and then drive sideways on Queen for six metres before getting back on Main once you were past the intersection. You stayed on Main while the other drivers stayed on Queen, except for the fact that you were both on the same bit of asphalt.

In the meantime, I wandered up and down the living room. Pacing was a habit I had started a lot of years ago. I would do it at school in order to make pretend that I had somewhere to be for the lunch hour. Of course, when I reached the end of the corridor I would just have to turn around and go back, but no one could accuse me of having nowhere to go. I was always moving in a direction, but the direction changed and I bounced back over and over again until the hour ended and I could go back to being forced into being somewhere. There was a safety in that; I could blame them for my existence in that space. During the in-between moments, though, I had nowhere to *be*. Anywhere I was seemed like the wrong place, and I couldn't just *sit there*. Even though people did that, I couldn't understand how they did. I couldn't just sit anywhere without staring at something, and then I couldn't stare at just anything. People were often offended if you were looking in the wrong direction, as if the direction of your look were invading their physical space. You had to look in a direction that could continue on past anything recognizable along its path, so as not to be accused of looking at anything in particular.

I stopped pacing and sat down to stretch. My hamstrings were always tight from sitting at desks. I used to get terrible leg cramps when I used to wear heels, but I had to stop. At some point, I had decided that that was enough. I wore the heels because they made my legs look longer and therefore more proportional to the relations in space I was *supposed* to manifest. When I wore the heels, my calves cramped up, and when my calves cramped up, the heels would keep them nice and tight, so that they didn't accidentally stretch out. That hurt like a bitch. Setting my foot heels down directly on the floor hurt for a while, but they eventually got used to it. The proportionality argument, it turned out, didn't work if I wanted to be out amongst other people. They didn't care if I maintained my proportionality as an independent entity if that meant that I wasn't proportional to them. Of course, there were some girls who liked to make a big deal out of my height;

they thought it made them seem smaller and there-fore cuter. Every girl wants to be someone else. The commonality between them is that they hate them-selves. I didn't get rid of the actual physical heels in the closet, though, for another ten years. After all, the occasion might arise for them to come out again.

The problem was the men. They hated the women, or they didn't, but they couldn't love them for any length of time. There was always something else, someone else, who seemed more interesting *after a while*. It was still a trope for there to be a long and detailed analysis of the early relationship between romantic partners. It was the "happily ever after" updated and starring the new woman-of-no-person-ality who really wanted to meet the right man, whose greatest quality was being inoffensive. If only I could find someone inoffensive, then life would be grand. If stories were going to be told ethically, I thought, they would have to adjust the focus so that the story's parts were proportional to the actual time spent living out the setup, the crisis, the climax, the conse-quences. When they got married it was supposed to stop time, but it didn't. You can't stop time with a legal document.

If they were going to tell *my* story, they would focus on day one, day two, day three (maybe) and then day four. And then it would be over. I wouldn't have to go through the actual time afterward, when it all seemed so already over. Everyone was supposed to have left the theatre on day four, but here they were living it out and carrying on.

The best weapon they had was consistency. If you did things enough times over, and in the same way, and around the same time, and you didn't wait long after the darkness set in, then you could effectively speed up time. Perhaps it was a form of self-hypnosis, like the factory worker who spends eight hours a day attaching part A to part B and then going home. How anyone could spend eight hours doing that, I thought, was amazing. But I also figured that, were I used to it, I could probably do it too. Something would happen to me such that it didn't seem as if the repetitions in time were piling up on one another, trying to bury me under parts A and B, but just streaming by like a river. And then you reached sixty-five and someone told you it was time to retire. You tell them that the past forty years seemed to fly by, you take the standard gift, and you go home. You say you don't know what you'll do with yourself but then, when you get home, things seem to pop up that take the days away. You don't know where the days have gone, and you remember a time when you used to be able to get up, go to work, run errands, feed yourself and do laundry, all in one day, when now it seems that night sneaks up on you as soon as you try to get anything done.

That was the answer; if you wanted more time, then do more things. At the same time, the people who were busy, who did all of the things, said they had no time. That was technically true; they had no *free* time, but the time in which they did things was longer. As I walked back and forth across the room, I wondered if that counted as a thing or not. I thought it did; it felt like it did. Time was moving slowly.

I wanted to go to the store to buy a box of crackers, the wheat crackers, the thin ones. I would have to pay extra at the corner store, but that meant I could go at night. The corner store would buy them from the grocery store during the day, double the price, and then sell them to me at night. I was glad to supplement the cracker price in exchange for the luxury of only having to go out at night. I thought that during the day, if I saw anyone, they might ask me what I was up to, and I might be honest. I was going home, again, to watch other people's lives on the television screen and eat crackers. In the worst telling of the story, they offered me an alternative thing to do in the evening, and I would either have to do it or explain to the person that I preferred crackers and television to whatever they were offering. It wasn't fair to make me choose between these two bad options, so I did what I could to avoid being placed in that position.

Of course I understood that there could be no proportionality with regard to the screen lives. I could go through months of a person's life in a single evening, if I focused on the relevant events, i.e., the ones that were relevant to whatever the point of the story was. A story that was proportional to how long life was would have to be as long as life itself, and that was unreasonable. Besides, people did a lot of boring things. Nobody watched the Attach Part A to Part B channel. Of course, you could watch that channel for a very long time, if it produced the same sort of hypnosis that the actual action induced.

If you eliminated temporal concerns, then people actually seemed to be good people. Someone could go away on a trip for three weeks, fall out of the picture, and return with gifts. We could assume that they did nothing important. That's not how humans behaved, though. They couldn't focus on anything. During the time that businessman was out of town, he probably felt the distance between himself and his wife grow ever temporally larger. Even when they spoke, she was far away, and while she usually knew exactly what he was up to at any given moment, she couldn't from *over there*. He had fulfilled his duty to his wife with a seven pm phone call, and he didn't have anything else to do with the evening, so he might as well find some hooker on the local website for that. It would be more than covered by his per diem.

That was one of the benefits of literature to film, I thought. Unless they used some tacky device like a narrator, it was impossible to fill a screen with the thoughts of people. People on the screen were like people you met in the world. They could go away and reappear, and you just filled in the missing time with nothingness. It wasn't as if you thought they failed to exist when they weren't on the screen. They existed, obviously, but what they were doing, nobody knew and it wasn't important. The people on the screen at any given time, you could only infer their thoughts through what they said and what they did. What they said and what they did gave no more insight into their thoughts than did the thoughts and speech of anyone else in the world.

The great irony of the thing is that you were supposed to access these people, these characters, their thoughts and lives and feelings, through the medium of people whose success depended on their ability to deceive you with regard to their thoughts and lives and feelings. If an actor could give you access to a character's thoughts and lives and feelings, it was only proof that anything you thought about another *person*'s thoughts and life and feelings (a real person) could very well be false. And it's not like people were honest.

I wasn't sure where I had gotten the idea first, but I remembered being convinced, during my formative years, that when people expressed a liking of me, they were enacting some kind of cruel joke at my expense. I remembered a boy who had told me he had liked me, and I had said, *yeah, right.* I didn't mean to be at the time, but I was probably appropriately cynical. He didn't like me. He liked that I was one of the few girls who seemed to dress in such a way as to garner male attention. That didn't mean he wasn't sincere, though. He was sincere. He really thought he did like me, and that my skirt was all there was to like about me. He was really sincere in that belief. I started to suspect that I was being overly suspicious when it kept happening. There was a turning point when a boy had called me for a date, and I had said I'd think about it (in order to take some time to determine if it was a sincere request or not), and after a couple of days he took the offer back. I decided I would have to infer, from then on, that even if someone were mistaken, they were at least sincere. And if they discovered that I had feelings, too, in addition to skirts, then so what. I was supposed to, right? What made it all right for other people and not for me?

I wondered if he had cheated that out of me. I couldn't remember having a sincere feeling. Maybe it was because I made an effort to destroy every positive image I had of something external to my control, in order to ensure that I wouldn't value it too highly only to have it lost. When he was around, I took every rejection as a sign of his value, as if his ability to fuck around with me meant that he could —he was allowed, for that's what he did. And if he was allowed, there must be some reason for that. And then there was the fact that he often used to tell me that no one would love me, except for him.

Maybe he meant that no one would ever love me like he did, like it was some kind of overestimation of his capacity to love, such that no one who didn't match it could feign love at all. Or maybe it was meant to describe that his love for me was of such an amplitude that corresponded to the fact that only he could understand how important I was and how valid my thoughts, so that no one else could comprehend my true value and love me accordingly. Or perhaps he was an asshole who was trying to destroy me so that I wouldn't leave him. It worked for a while.

Another one of his tactics would be to claim that he was going to kill himself if I didn't do X—if I didn't come over, if I didn't tell off that other guy who seemed interested, if I didn't whatever. The reason I held out for so long, I thought, is because I couldn't ethically abandon him without having reached the point where I didn't give a fuck if he lived or died. That was how it was, by the end.

Not very long had passed at all, by the time I had thought all these thoughts. It was getting darker, but it wasn't clear that it was dark enough to be considered dark, or if it were just the period in which people still pretended it was day.

It must be dark, there he is, I thought first. It didn't make any sense; it was just an expression of how I was thinking one thing and then anything, and then formed some causal relation between them. It wasn't as if he always showed up exactly when the darkness turned dark.

Outside, through the kitchen window, I could see him. There was a large tree in the middle of the backyard that made it useless for most backyard activities. I could only grow plants that thrived in the shade, and no sort of lawn furniture of planned out arrangement was meant to fit around its massive trunk. There were a couple of ways it could be removed. If I wanted to make the ground flat, they would have to dig around it and then cut the roots off individually as they crawled out through the rest of the lawn from the centre. A lot of them would be quite substantial, and that would take a lot of effort. The whole thing would have to be removed piece by piece.

There was an easier way, though, where they would still have to remove the above ground tree parts piece by piece, but they could stop when they had a sizeable trunk leftover, and just leave it. It would make an interesting patio table, I thought, if only people didn't want to put their legs under it. If people wanted to sit around a tree trunk table with their knees awkwardly off to the side, then that would be fine. They would adjust. I thought women would look better sitting around this table than the men would, with their knees off to the side.

At this moment, from the lowest hanging branch, he hung. He hung there and hung there, as if he didn't have anything better to do. I thought he might not. I had never figured out what he had gone on to do with his life, but I knew that at some point he had meant to attend medical school. That would have been a disaster, I thought. He can't even stay alive right himself. Had he done anything of note, I should have been able to find that out, but all of my investigations had turned up nothing. He had either done nothing, or he had done nothing because he had been dead for quite a while.

But he hadn't been. He had just gotten there. I should have been surprised, I thought, and so I made some motions as if I were surprised. There was no one there to see, but it was best to keep in the habit.

I went out back and looked at him. For a while, I just looked at him. I made a systematic scan from bit to bit, checking for inconsistencies. He was just as he should have been, I thought. The human body was all four elements at once—solid, liquid, gas, and fire. It was pretty cold out, so he would be cold soon too. I checked to see if he had goosebumps, but he didn't. He could have, I thought, if it was cold when he died and if they froze quickly enough in place, but apparently not.

He was just barely not touching the ground, and he had put the rope so close to the tree trunk, it was as if he didn't want to venture too far out for fear of hanging himself. Maybe it was an accident, then. Maybe I was meant to see him out there, take pity on him, and commit the rest of my life to making up for all of his inadequacies as a human, putting his transitory feelings over and above any of mine, and always trying to make sure he was pleased so that he wouldn't go and do something like this. I was glad to have arrived too late to have to consider any other options.

He wore a shirt with a pocket; that was unusual. It wasn't the same shirt that I remembered him wearing, sometimes day after day. Maybe he was coming home from a recital, or an interview, or a funeral, I thought, and smiled a little. I was supposed to notice the shirt and the fact that it had a pocket. The human body was full of holes and then people added more holes onto the outside, because the ones they already had weren't fit for many external objects or, if you attempted to carry anything around in them, they would get wet and you would look weird. No, the pocket was meant to be noticed. It appeared to me in the same style as that bit of the scenery in the old cartoons that you knew was about to move because it was shaded differently than the rest of the surrounding scenery. The pocket was about to move. I put my hand in it and felt for the note. (Of course there was a note in it.)

"Dear _____, I can't live without you."

I wondered what had gone on in his funny head that made him think that he *could* live *with* me. Perhaps he wanted a roommate, and I was the only one who would do. He couldn't live with me though, because I had cats and he was allergic, so he had to kill himself. Perhaps he was supposed to live in the same complex, but the superintendent found out about his balcony windmill collection and, for the safety of the other tenants, made him choose between living near me or the windmills. He couldn't live without either of these, so he had to kill himself. Of course that's not what the note said. Everyone knew that it implied that if only I were to live with him, as in doom myself for the rest of time in no such happily ever after, then he would be fine and try not to die as best he could. I basically owed it to him, the viewers would think. But that was not the case, and it was completely irrational to think so.

According to the rules of logic, you could not contrapose a negative statement and turn it into a conditional. "I can't live without you" did not mean that "If you were with me, I could live." That was an additional inference that everyone made that I would have to cite now as a formal fallacy, if anyone gave me any trouble. What was logical to infer: "I can live with you" (if you believed in the idea that double negatives made positives); "I can't live without you or

I'm about to die" (you could turn anything into a disjunct, and if the first part were true the whole thing would be true); if the subject "I" didn't exist, then also "I *can* live without you" but only because he was dead. It wasn't meant to indicate anything positive.

He couldn't live without me, because he couldn't do anything at all. "Dead men tell no tales" was not only a cliché but a trivial bit of nonsense that made a very specific statement about something about which *every* negative statement was true. Dead men also don't eat breakfast; they don't hate telephones; and they don't vacuum the carpet often enough.

"I can live with you" could be truncated to "I can live," I thought. The "with you" part didn't necessarily specify that the living was restricted to the scenario where it was conditional on this and only this condition being met. Was it a necessary or a sufficient condition? He was trying to make it seem as if it were a sufficient condition, as if I was all he needed to live. That, of course, was wrong. He obviously also needed air.

There was a definite time concern as well. I was obviously meant to read the note and place it in time relative to some previous hour when he was alive to write it. Of course, he should have known that I wouldn't read it until after he was dead. And if I were reading it after he was dead, then obviously he couldn't live without me. He couldn't live at all he couldn't live without me, or in a tree, or with syphilis. If a dead man had written it, then the note meant nothing at all. It depended on whether you believed that the man who wrote the note was the same one who was now dead, or if you believed that the man who wrote the note was the one who was formerly alive. The difference mattered, logically.

I didn't know if it warranted calling the emergency number, since there was nothing to do now about it. I didn't know the regular police number, though. Perhaps I should be calling the hospital, so that they could pick him up and bring him to the morgue. That might indicate to them that I was responsible for the corpse, though. I didn't want that. So I found and called the police number. I thought if I hung up quickly enough, they wouldn't be able to discern what my feelings were about the situation. So I called the number, waited for someone alive to answer the call, and simply said, "There's a dead guy in my yard." I figured they would trace the call and arrive soon. I might tell them that I was so broken up about it that I forgot to mention the address. It didn't matter.

TEN

THE WORST PART about cleaning was the worst part about driving. There was nothing to think about. That's why I always put it off. Of course, when you actually started cleaning, you realized there was no such task as general *cleaning*. There were particular verbs that *cleaning* corresponded to—scrubbing, rinsing, wiping, turning water on and off, all of which I forgot existed whenever it was time to start actually *cleaning*. What solved the problem were also those particulars—the fact that when I actually started cleaning something, I could divide the task into so many subtasks and along the way feel a growing sense of accomplishment. The same was true of walking. I always avoided walking, because then I would have too much time to think. But when I actually did it—cross the road here without getting hit by cars, navigate this ditch, keep to the edge of the asphalt, where the sun reflected the least harshly. With all of the subtasks, it didn't seem like anything at all. The purpose wasn't to *clean* the bathtub; it was to remove the pink from around the drain with a sponge and that bleach cleaner. That way, if my scrubbing were a little lackluster, at least I could be reasonably certain that anything there would be dead.

I went at the bathroom first. The bathroom always felt the best once it was done. There was a clean scent that went along with it, and it was relatively quick. Then, I would either isolate the bathroom as being the clean area of the house, or I would start noticing that everything else seemed not as clean in comparison, and I would continue cleaning for as long as it took to get the job done.

I knew what it was like to have no other options than to get the job done. That wasn't the troublesome part. I always looked strangely at people when they said that they had to miss one thing for another, or put off this thing for that thing, or prioritize things in their life because they had decided that blank and X and the other was just too much. Those people didn't know what it was like to have no other options than to get the job done. And they would say stupid things, like *I couldn't get it done*. You *could have*, I thought in most cases. It was within the realm of possibility, but you've somehow been socialized to believe that it was acceptable to let some of your responsibilities fall off the radar when some other appeared as an excuse. Once you started doing it, I guessed that you believed that you literally *couldn't* do everything expected of you, but the people who believed that had no idea what it was like to have no other options than to get the job done.

I had had an English teacher in high school—secondary school. Mrs. Nielson was always late with the grading. Students would harass her for their grades, and she would try to explain by telling them that *she had kids*. Who gives a fuck, woman, lots of people have kids. It's not unusual to have kids, and having them doesn't excuse you from your responsibilities to other people—assuming you actually consented to having those responsibilities. In the case of an English teacher, I thought that would definitely apply. I had had a lot of responsibilities, though, to which I hadn't consented. Still, I had gotten the job done.

People did not understand, and by understand here, I mean have compassion for. If you demonstrated some weakness, that was room to move in. That was something to use against you, and anyone and everyone *would* use it against you. People demonstrated compassion when they thought that there would be some eventual benefit. Usually, that would be a reciprocated compassion, defined in the sense of how other people would allow you to make such sorry excuses for your self-imposed incapacities, but not always.

I didn't know how to conceive of this particular responsibility. There was a job that had to be done, but I was sure that I hadn't consented to do it, even though I had been the principal actor in the creation of said responsibility. This was what people meant when they said that something happened "against their will." I thought that people too often used that as an excuse to deny responsibility. If they didn't take care of it, though, that meant that the task would fall to someone else. And that someone else usually had even less responsibility for whatever had to be done. There were some things you just couldn't get out of by claiming that you hadn't caused them. Whether you had caused them or not didn't matter, a lot of the time. Sometimes, there was just a job to be done and someone who had to do it, and tonight I was that someone.

I thought I had handled it relatively well so far.

He had shown up at the door relatively late into the evening. I figured that he had had a full day of activities, had decided on a leisurely dinner, and then perhaps after a couple of drinks he had decided to stop by. It was weird to picture him having any drinks at all. He was far too young to have had any drinks when I had known him. Of course, it stood to reason that since he had aged a couple of decades since then, he had since been introduced to alcohol and all of its fine benefits. Back then he was excited to get those chocolate covered coffee beans; they were as hard a drug as he did back then. Or perhaps he had decided not to drink at all. He had gone to that camp, and they had probably told him that alcohol was the devil's sweat-juice, or whatever seemed most terrifying at the time, and he had been a teetotaler ever since. Or maybe he was one of those people who claimed that he never drank, except when anyone offered him a drink or he felt like one. That sounded most like him. That would fit the best. When I pictured him taking a drink he still looked the same as he did back then—a skinny but broad-shouldered teenager with dark blond, close-cropped curly hair, dimples and bags around his eyes from not sleeping, never sleeping. Perhaps the alcohol helped with that, although it never did for me.

He did sleep, though. I could still hear him yelling about how terrible a time he had of it, only getting to sleep seven hours a night. He blamed his poor mother for that. When I was young I had hated his mother as much as he did. I believed everything he said about her, including everything that didn't make sense. She was, after all, the crazy lady on Earl Street, but in the years since I had come to understand. He was just being a dick. He was always being a dick, and it was always someone else's fault. I tried to remember the last time I had slept for seven hours straight. At the time I hadn't really kept track of how many hours I slept—it had always seemed like enough. I didn't have to micromanage the whole system with various sorts of sedatives, each of which lost effect with too much use and gained effect with careful periods of abstention. On a good night, I might get seven hours. That was enough, I thought, to get the job done.

I didn't feel tired at all, and that was to be expected. He had disrupted my evening by showing up like that, and I couldn't go through the usual process. There were processes, but they were unusual. I couldn't go to sleep until at least the bathroom was clean.

He looked pathetic, standing there outside. I had peered through the blinds to see who would be knocking. I figured it was probably the neighbour again. The neighbour knew I lived alone and would sometimes come with reports about the neighbourhood when a strange car stayed too long or if anything else seemed out of sorts. He would come and check to make sure that I was all right. I thought he worried about me, and that seemed to be all right so far. I figured that it was some kind of fatherly affection. He used to have a family, but they hated him, he had told me once. I didn't inquire as to why. I assumed that he thought there was something to make up for, and by letting him give his briefings, I could contribute to that in some small way. He was a little late today, but that wasn't completely unusual. There were sometimes very pressing matters that he simply had to investigate immediately—did I recognize the bicycle left against the side of the house? Was my car being repaired, loaned out, or had somebody stolen it? Did I have anyone to help clean the eavestroughs, or could he help me find somebody?

I assumed, of course, that he would eventually try to fuck me, fatherly feeling or not, and that he would grow immediately unconcerned when I had to reject him. Or did I have to? Yes. I used to think that it was easier to fuck them and get it over with. But that was never the end of it. If you fucked them once, they expected you to again, and then they expected you to shack up and bear their subpar children, so that if you didn't want to end up the broodmare of some genetically inferior male, then you'd better not even look at them with anything but contempt. Nothing as terrible as fucking him would happen as a result of the rejection. Of course, I had to account for the fact that he knew all of my habits, when I was home, when I was not home, where the extra key was, and I also had to account for that fact that I knew that men often went batshit crazy when they were rejected. It would be my fault for failing to appreciate him and all he's done for me, and god knows what would happen then. Maybe there was a really good reason his family hated him.

Having peered through the blinds, though, my visitor now knew I was home, and my neighbour was nowhere. I didn't consider until much later the option that I had to just admit I was home and not answer the door. It just hadn't come to mind. I had either the option of pretending not to be home or of answering the door, and I had implicitly given up the first option by peering through the blinds, so I thought. I froze. I knew I was doing it, and that it would seem odd, and that the longer I stared, the more certain he would be of his perception of me peering through the blinds. The longer I did it, the less I could pretend that I was a stranger and that _____ had moved out some time before. I considered simultaneously how rude it was of me to leave people standing outside when I knew they were there and they knew I was home. Those were just good manners. There had to be some pretty extreme circumstances to allow for the deviation from good manners, the foundations of civil society.

I thought about quickly texting a friend to tell them that he was here, and that if anything happened to me... but then I thought that they might text back, and then he would see the previous text on the screen and that it would set him off, and I would have in essence ensured my own demise. He was standing outside rather patiently; he hadn't yelled through the door yet to see what was the matter with me, why wasn't I opening it. He stood there, half expecting to be turned away, I guessed. *All right, then.* If he half expected that, then it seemed that his going away was an option. And if his going away was an option, then there was no reason I shouldn't open the door.

"Hello," I said.

"Hello."

"What are you doing here?"

Now I waited. If he were the same as he was before, he would have a whole speech prepared. He would have come up with a list of reasons why I owed it to him to listen, and what he thought should happen from now on. He would take stock of the situation and determine what particular actions I would have to take in order to fit into his plan, and he would insist that I get on with it right away. But that didn't happen, so he wasn't the same as before. Perhaps there was nothing to be afraid of.

I used to keep a knife in my purse, just in case he turned up again. I needed a knife that I was allowed to use, that I knew well, that only I knew existed. Withholding information became a form of control for me, and the worse he was at anticipating my thoughts and actions, the better off I thought I was. The distance wasn't spatial or temporal but *epistemic*. If I shut up and allowed him to believe whatever he wanted to believe, then I could, whenever I wanted, speak up and contradict him. *No!* I would say. *You assumed X based on Y, but X isn't true and I've known it all along!* That was some small victory. Of course, what usually happened is that I went along with him, pretending that X was X and X was true, because it seemed the easiest and safest way to deal with him.

The door opened directly into the living room. There was no buffer zone where I could hold him if I wanted to. I imagined living in a much larger house, where there would be a foyer with three inte-rior doors. I would answer the door by entering the foyer from any one of the three doors, but upon entering the foyer I would close the door again, not allowing the visitor to see what was behind the other two. Perhaps I was behind one door, while the other doors held rabid wolves that only responded to a kill command in another language.

Had he had a dog? I suddenly couldn't remem-ber. I had a vague recollection of him telling me a story about teaching a dog a German kill command.

I didn't know any German at the time and was very impressed. But I couldn't remember what the dog *looked* like. It could have been a German Shepherd, but it was just as likely I was filling in that detail because of my vague recollection of that story. I was reasonably certain that the story came from my memory of actual events and not anything I had seen in a movie or on television, because the anecdote dwindled off into nothing, just like actual interactions did. It was possible that he had a dog and that the dog was always downstairs with his mother, while he preferred to host me in his room upstairs. Now, I thought, the story of the German kill command was probably a lie. Perhaps someone had told the same lie to him, or perhaps it was an inside joke within his family. In any case, I couldn't remember if the dog existed, and imagining the details only made me more suspect that I could imagine as many details as I liked and remember much more than used to exist.

So I had let him in, and there he was, all the way in the living room. There was a small area where he could stand without dirtying the carpet with his shoes, so perhaps social structures would prevent him from coming in any farther. Of course, the polite thing to do would be to tell him to take off his shoes and the invite him to take a seat and offer him a beverage. I didn't, for a while. I wanted to see first if he might just go away without causing any trouble. I didn't go to the doctor very often, because I knew that a lot of common ailments would just go away on their own, and I reasoned that the same might be true of him. And of course, it would be rude to let him just stand there. Perhaps if I offered him a seat then he would refuse, state the reason for his visit, and then leave me alone. Perhaps if I didn't offer him a seat he would continue to stand there, and he would never state his purpose or leave.

He would just stand in the small area just inside the door not speaking, forever. I would grow used to him eventually, although it would be terribly awkward trying to open and close the door around him. I pictured myself hitting him with it, accidentally on purpose, because he got in the way, was always in the way, and never seemed to take a hint that maybe it was time to leave. He had been there so many years now, it was time to leave. He didn't need food or water to continue to exist, just the opportunity to now and then get in the way of my opening the door. That seemed to be enough for him.

But that was the future. For now, he had been standing in the little area for a little longer than felt appropriate, and I thought that offering him a seat without telling him to take his shoes off might give him the hint he needed. Instead, he bent over and started undoing his laces. I thought he might have at least had the decency to wear shoes without laces, so I didn't have to stare at his dandruffy balding scalp as he bent over to untie his shoes. I could see buttcrack at the top of jeans below his jacket, and he obviously didn't bend over that often. He seemed uncomfortable doing it, like it was too far, like he was used to some more comfortable arrangements for putting on and taking off shoes. I looked at him doing that so awkwardly and resented him for making it seem as though my doorway and its location in the house were insufficient to his habits.

Eventually he stood back up, some sweat drops on his forehead from the effort. I hoped they didn't fall on the floor. I didn't want them in the air, either. Everything about him was invasive, and he didn't leave a single element in my house untouched. He kept breathing the air and allowing his sweat to evaporate, and he was taking up the space, all of which I required.

I knew that if I lived somewhere smaller, I would get used to it. But I had gotten used to this space, and now I required all of it. If I acquired any physical things, then something else had to go. I needed the extra space to think in, and when there was too much in it, I couldn't think things as clearly as I might have without all of that interference. He counted as a thing, and I couldn't figure out how to move around him or where to place myself in relation. He had thrown everything off with his materiality; he was taking up all of the space.

If he got to the chair, he would soak into it. The sweat would come off of him and into the wooden chair, and then I would have to get rid of that too. That was the risk of having porous furniture, though, the fact that it would receive substances from the environment. Usually I didn't think much of it. Usually I didn't have him trying to get into my space, breathing my air. I would have to open the windows too.

Eventually he stood up and, even though he looked more pathetic than anybody I'd ever seen, seemed to have all of the confidence in the world of his right to be there and his right to speak.

"We have to talk."

"I had assumed you had some such purpose."

"We have to talk about us. I'm still not over it. There must be a reason."

"What reason do you think that is?"

"That we're meant to be together."

"Not some failure on your part?"

Of course it was some failure on his part. I didn't even think he was being honest, though. He thought, now, that there had been some enduring feeling on his part, and he probably imagined that it had remained there, consistently present for twenty years or so, and that the only explanation for that phenomenon was the fact that there was some fate acting on him in order to make his earthly purpose known to him so that he might finally show up at my house at a semi-inappropriate hour to live out his destiny. The reasoning would have been sound, if he hadn't just made up all the fucking premises.

I was certain, absolutely certain, that if he were honest with himself, he would reflect on the past twenty years, add up all of the moments in which he didn't think about me at all, realize that they dwarfed the moments in which he actually did remember me, albeit inaccurately, and then come to the reasonable conclusion that this, too, was a momentary feeling that only persisted long enough for him to actually show up at my door for the fact that he was already on his way. It was easy to continue being in motion if you were already in motion, and then to explain to yourself that the continuing motion remained focused on the initial goal, even though what was really going on was human inertia.

People, like things, did stuff, just because it seemed like the next thing to do, and people could delete the intermediate time it took to perform those actions, rationalizing that the intermediate moments were all unified under some umbrella goal that prevented them from getting reality all over themselves. Reality was the moments in between, where if you weren't careful, you might think that your goal was just *to clean* and not to make sure to scrub next to the sink fixtures to get all the crud out (well, almost all of it).

His goal was to clean, or in this case, to do something abstract, something that would eliminate the intermediate time and result in a satisfying stasis. It was really unreasonable, and why he thought I might have owed it to him to pretend was beyond me. I grew more offended by the idea, the longer I stared at him and the closer he got to my furniture.

I couldn't push him through the window. He wasn't angled properly, and then everyone would hear the noise. The neighbour would come over to report that the window was broken. He would see that I had a man in the house, feel betrayed, and delete all of the pictures he had found of me on the internet that he kept in a special masturbation folder. He wouldn't die, and though he might go away for a while, I would have to see him again, if only because of the insurance claim he would file due to the accident that took place on my property. Of course it was an accident.

I didn't know what had happened to the knife. I imagined that, perhaps, I had put it in a drawer with the rest of the cutlery, and then donated it somewhere accidentally. I liked to get new things when I moved to a new place, and although sometimes I ended up missing something I had previously gotten rid of, I didn't miss anything enough to regret getting rid of the rest. He was kind of the same. I knew that anything I did miss about him would be a tiny moment in amongst a temporal sea of bullshit and that I couldn't just choose one and leave the rest. You couldn't choose to ignore the hundreds of times that a dog had bitten you and remember the one time that it didn't. It was an apple-cutting knife, I used to say, so I had probably put it in the cutlery drawer at some point, and now it was gone. Of course, there were other knives in the cutlery drawer. Would it be odd to go cut apples? Probably.

So no windows, and no apples. Someone had to make a computer joke about that, I thought, and I smiled. He thought I was smiling at him.

"So you think so too?" he asked.

"No, I don't."

His face changed a little. I could see a bit of the old him in there, the thing that came out when I contradicted him.

"I've thought a lot about this; I think you'd change your mind if you just let me explain."

"No, I don't think so."

"How can you say that? You don't even know what I'm going to say."

That was only trivially true. I could guess the general form of what he was going to say. I could guess that he would remember something incorrectly, ascribe some importance to something else that wasn't really all that important, and then claim that in the face of such a body of evidence you couldn't help but come to the conclusion that I was being unreasonable not to agree with him. Perhaps it was some failure on *my* part. Perhaps I didn't *understand* what he was saying, and he would just have to explain and explain until I did. There really was no other option, I thought. There was no way to convince him that he was wrong, because anything I said would be interpreted as the kind of thing one would say if they didn't *understand*. If I would just *let* him explain, he could clear up this confusion I was having, and then once I *understood*, I would agree with him, because god fucking damn it there was no motherfucking possible way he was just fucking wrong. He had *thought* about it, for fuck's sake.

It was too late not to let him in. He couldn't go through the window, and he probably wouldn't die if he did, because we were on the ground floor. I couldn't take the apple knife from the apple drawer. I thought about the board game where you had to guess the murder weapon and the room it took place in. I was playing the same kind of game, except that I knew what room it would be; I just had to find something suitable to do it with. The candlesticks had gone with the rest of the boxes of old dishes in the last move. Or maybe I had put those in storage. It didn't matter; they weren't *here*. If I were smart, I would have gotten one of those jobs that didn't advertise the fact that you worked for them all over the internet, by which I meant on their website and only on their website. He wouldn't have found anything when he searched for me, and I could have pretended to be dead.

There was a hand weight in the coat closet. I knew it. There were two of them. I had taken them with me to an aerobics class during the trial week when I didn't have to pay, and then I had put them down in the closet on my way in the door and left them there. So unless the universe decided to fuck with me, there was a hand weight in the coat closet. And I could get it, if only he was so caught up in his own melodrama that he assumed, for about ten seconds, that when I went for the closet, I was trying to do anything *but* find a weapon. I made for the closet, trying to exude the vibe of a person who had just decided that since company had come over, I had better tidy up a bit. I rummaged on the floor for a few seconds, and then I felt a hand on my shoulder. It yanked me back so hard that I hit my tailbone on the floor and felt a searing nerve pain.

Why won't you listen to what I have to say. I wasn't sure if I made up the voice or if I actually heard it; the two kinds of thing didn't seem all that separate at the moment. Surely, people could hear imaginary things and imagine hearing things. What was important was that when I fell back, I maintain a hard grip on the hand weight. It was the most important thing now, more important than the pain and more important than the hand. The hand was just a placeholder, and I tried to calculate based on where the hand had come from where the head should be. If I waited too long the head could move. I prayed to whatever gods Ajax had prayed to in the *Iliad* that my shot ring true.

He was bleeding. That would take a while to get out of the carpet. He wasn't bleeding enough, though. *Hey*, I thought I heard, and I wasn't sure if it was him or the shock I imagined he felt when he realized he wasn't in control here. This wasn't his space. He seemed to feel the right to exist wherever he was, but he didn't account for the fact that this would leave him with a tactical disadvantage.

As I tried to hit him again, though, he grabbed my wrist. For a second or longer, it seemed like a stalemate. I would hold on to the hand weight for as long as it took, and he would hold on to my wrist for the same amount of time. It wasn't a stalemate, though. He twisted my arm and all at once, I was on the ground. I would have rugburn on my chin, I thought, from the awkward angle I had hit. I was on the ground, and he had both arms.

No. No. It was just like old times. He grabbed my other arm, at first with two hands, one hand per wrist, and then he forced them together so that he could hold both wrists with one of his hands. I couldn't seem to move enough to get out of it, and now I was facedown with both wrists behind my back. He put his knee on my tailbone to keep me from using my knees to prop myself up, and the pain seared again. Now it seemed I was in for it.

Play dead, I thought. That was for bears. It probably wouldn't work here. Besides, who knew what he had been into in the interim years. Maybe he was a serial murderer who stalked women who looked like me, who got off on necrophilia, and this was going to be his shining moment. More importantly, though, it wouldn't work. He felt around for the buttons on the front of my pants and found them. Even though it took him a while to figure it out, he didn't have to rush. I wasn't going anywhere. I willed my vagina to close, to become a nothing between my legs such that if he tried to poke at it, all he would find was a closed off bit of skin like a doll, no way in. It would have to close up the entire length, though. If it only closed at the end, he might force his way through anyway. Once he had read that it was possible to thrust himself up through my cervix, and he did his damnedest to try out his new sex trick. Damn, did that hurt.

My body betrayed me again. My vagina didn't close up, and he pinned me down, one hand on my wrists, the other on the back of my head, his knees on my thighs. Without using his hand to help, it took him a while to find his way in, but he made it work.

Every failure was terrible, and he was a terrible human.

Maybe if I pretended to like it, he would finish more quickly. No, I thought, he would just pretend that he wanted to draw it out, because he *loved* me, and he wanted to *make love* to me. It was fucking disgusting, the words he used. There was nothing they corresponded to, nothing they said, nothing they *meant*. I tried not to focus on the weave of the carpet in my face and instead on ways to hurt him. I could think of many ways I would like to hurt him, but none of them seemed practicable.

Until I remembered. Once, I had been trying to get it over with, some guy from a bar I thought might be easier to get rid of if I let him fuck me. So I did. But he was drunk and taking too long, so I got on top where I could ride him and also fondle around his balls and perineum, hopefully to make things go a little more quickly. But I had bent back too far, and he had cried out in pain. I knew it wasn't true of all men, that if you bent it too far down it would hurt, but *some*, and I thought he might be one of them. What I needed to do was determine the best point of contact with the floor from which to make my attack, the greatest source of static friction on which to anchor myself. From my anchor, I would thrust myself as best I could downward, hopefully hurting him. With my hands behind my back, my shoulders didn't touch the floor or, at least, they couldn't be trusted as a pivot. Since I was trying for a downward force, my toes wouldn't work either. It would have to be my face. The chin already hurt from when I went down, and I thought it might not provide enough surface area anyway, for the amount of friction I wanted to generate. If I could just exert enough upward force with *my whole face*, then the reactive force of the floor would force my body downward, and hopefully I would hurt him.

I did.

For a second he let go of me, in order to grab at his own genitals, and I took that moment to take back my hand weight. I would be better off with the twenty pound one, I thought, but I only had five pounds. Still, at least I had five pounds. Some of those women used weights that were one pound, or even half a pound. I couldn't imagine being able to tell the difference. I hit him wherever I could, hopefully the face. If I could disable his perceptual organs, he wouldn't be able to tell where I was, and then I could more easily hit him some more. I hit him, and I hit him, and the motion started to take on a rhythm that made the time pass more quickly from moment to moment. If I weren't careful, I thought, I could put in a whole shift of hitting him, and then pass the responsibility on to someone else for another eight hours.

I hit him and hit him. I had had several dreams about hitting him, just like this one, except in my dreams whenever I tried to hit him, I didn't seem able to exert any force. I would wake up frustrated about the fact that I had him, I had him and I hit him, and no matter what, my punches would land with no force. I decided it must be a dream thing. This was different. I was definitely having some effect, but not as much as I might like, or not as quickly. Still, I had a job to do, and it had to be done. There was no other option than to get the job done.

I would shower first, and then he would, and then I would clean up. That's how it would be done. I shut off the downstairs lights so that I might drag him upstairs; who knows what shadows I might cast on the front blinds if I didn't. I could navigate well in the dark, and he seemed to be taking up less of my space now that he wasn't taking in all of the air. He was like a heavy bit of furniture that seemed out of place when first acquired, but grew to be part of the environment over time. Except he couldn't stay there; he wasn't furniture. Furniture didn't disintegrate like he would. If I didn't take care of the problem, and quickly, then he would start to smell, and if my house smelled, someone might think I didn't make the efforts I did to keep it clean. I wasn't the *best* housekeeper, but my house didn't *smell*. I knew that I would need another shower when I was done, but in the meantime, I wanted this one. I left him outside the bathroom so he couldn't see. I would need to clean the carpet, too, before I went to bed, all the way from the front closet to the upstairs bathroom. If the bleach cleaner ruined the carpet, it didn't matter much.

What was important was that he get in the shower. I put him in and turned it on. I started cleaning everything around him first. If I did the small jobs first, then I would get into cleaning mode, and the bigger tasks I had left until the end would seem smaller. So I cleaned the mirror and took everything off of the shelves so I could clean them too. Top to bottom, I thought. That was how I had been taught—to start cleaning from the highest vertical point, because as I cleaned some of the dirt or dust would inevitably fall to the lower points. So I might as well leave those until last. Then I would clean the mirror and the shelves, the sink and toilet, and leave the bathtub until last. I set him in there and turned it on, because I thought that it might be easier to clean him if he soaked a while. That, and I thought that whatever he was, I could reduce his concentration by mixing him with water. I had learned that sometimes it didn't matter *how much* of a substance there was, but what mattered was the *concentration* it existed in. One part bleach undiluted would work better than ten parts bleach diluted to one tenth. The same amount of bleach existed, but the first would work better. Of course, if I were running low on bleach, I might water it out some, because it was easier to spread ten parts bleach to all of the parts I needed to spread it to than it was to spread one part. I wasn't running low on bleach, though.

I poured some into the water. It was going to be hell on my hands, but I could always wear the rubber gloves. I didn't think they were all that effective, though, since I always ended up putting my hands into the water farther than the gloves reached, so that the bleach water would get inside them and they would act as a way of confining it to my hands instead of as a barrier. He wasn't diluting visibly, so I had to think of a way to speed things up. I had quite a few implements for getting rid of unwanted body parts—my own— like skin and hair and nails. Bones would be tough, I thought, but maybe someone had invented a way to get rid of those too. *The ultimate beauty product—slough off unwanted bones with our bone laser-twister-peeler*. I laughed. I would have to deal with those later.

I couldn't deal with any large parts yet anyway, because it was my intention that anything that could go down the drain would go down the drain. So I started picking away at little bits of flesh here and there, trying to make the bits small enough so that I wouldn't need to use any drain cleaner when I was done. I shouldn't have poured the bleach in the water, I thought, if I then had to use drain cleaner. The bleach would neutralize it, and all of the hair in the drain would remain undissolved. *Best to keep to small bits.* The bleach gave off a scent of cleanliness, and I felt good about the fact that every time a bit was removed, I could dip it back in the bleach water so that I was always touching a sterile surface. Bit by bit by bit he went.

I didn't know how long it would take—a very long time, by my own estimate. That was the thing, though. It was one of those situations where I *couldn't* just give up. There was no other option than to get the job done. That's what most people didn't understand. I imagined some lesser being on the news, explaining how they had tried to get rid of the body, but had given up after such and such a time because it was just *too hard*. *Too hard* was supposed to be some definite point on a spectrum of difficulty that allowed one to give up on their responsibilities and to declare them someone else's problem. They would say nothing of the sort about me. He was going down the drain.

Acknowledgments

Thanks to Leza Cantoral and Christoph Paul at CLASH Books. Your enthusiasm for this book and your appreciation of all things philosophical mean a lot, and I'll be forever grateful for your support. Thanks also to Chandra Wohleber, for your comments on the manuscript and for your book recommendations. Finally, thanks to Rob Luzecky, for always telling me that whatever I've written is the best thing I've ever written.

About the Author

Charlene Elsby, Ph.D., is the Philosophy Program Director in the Department of English and Linguistics at Purdue University Fort Wayne. HEXIS is her first novel. Follow her on Twitter @ElsbyCharlene

Also by CLASH Books

TRAGEDY QUEENS: STORIES INSPIRED BY LANA DEL REY & SYLVIA PLATH

Edited by Leza Cantoral

GIRL LIKE A BOMB

Autumn Christian

CENOTE CITY

Monique Quintana

99 POEMS TO CURE WHATEVER'S WRONG WITH YOU OR CREATE THE PROBLEMS YOU NEED

Sam Pink

TIIIS BOOK IS BROUGHT TO YOU BY MY STUDENT LOANS

Megan J. Kaleita

PAPI DOESN'T LOVE ME NO MORE

Anna Suarez

ARSENAL/SIN DOCUMENTOS

Francesco Levato

THIS IS A HORROR BOOK

Charles Austin Muir

TRY NOT TO THINK BAD THOUGHTS

Art by Matthew Revert

SEQUELLAND

Jay Slayton-Joslin

JAH HILLS

Unathi Slasha

NEW VERONIA

M.S. Coe

**THE HAUNTING OF THE PARANORMAL
ROMANCE AWARDS**

Christoph Paul & Mandy De Sandra

COMAVILLE

Kevin Bigley

DARK MOONS RISING IN A STARLESS NIGHT

Mame Bougouma Diene

**IF YOU DIED TOMORROW I WOULD EAT
YOUR CORPSE**

Wrath James White

HORROR FILM POEMS

Poetry by Christoph Paul & Art by Joel Amat Güell

NIGHTMARES IN ECSTASY

Brendan Vidito

WE PUT THE LIT IN
LITERARY

CLASHBOOKS.COM

FOLLOW US ON TWITTER, IG & FB

@clashbooks

EMAIL

clashmediabooks@gmail.com

Printed in the USA
CPSIA information can be obtained
at www.ICGtesting.com
JSHW020828110624
64551JS00006B/446

9 781944 866525